Man in The Pandemic

A.F. Winter

TKOIC Publishing

SUMMERVILLE, SOUTH CAROLINA

Copyright © 2021 by **A.F. Winter**

TKOIC Publishing
P.O. Box 114
Summerville, SC 29484
www.afwinter.com

Publisher's Note: This is a work of fiction. Names, characters, places, and incidents are a product of the author's imagination. Locales and public names are sometimes used for atmospheric purposes. Any resemblance to actual people, living or dead, or to businesses, companies, events, institutions, or locales is completely coincidental.

Man in the Pandemic / A.F. Winter. -- 1st ed.
ISBN 978-1-7367793-0-9

To Phyllis Rothman, my mother's dear friend
And Seymour Coven, my uncle.
Both were a wonderful part of my childhood.

Dedicated to my dog Millie, without whose
company this might be a work of nonfiction.

DAY ONE

before the sun i rise
i make my bed
and go to work
i work
– A. Summer

Frank Smith was unremarkable in every way. He prided himself on being average. Average weight, average height, average hair color. Even his name was average.

He was not the kind of person to show off. He wore black framed glasses, the cheapest kind that were available.

He flew under the radar. He kept his cards close to the vest. His mother used to say, "If you show off, you'll attract the evil eye!"

Frank did not believe in evil eyes, but just in case, there was no harm in being safe.

The only time that Frank Smith failed was when he tried to do something above average. And so, he tried never to excel. All he wanted to be was a nice guy. No one ever felt threatened by him; he was too nice. But if you never stick out, you are never remembered, either.

So Frank Smith was sent home in the first wave during the first days of the pandemic to work remotely. The office had a quick meeting to review work-at-home procedures and then everyone left.

Frank smiled when he opened his door. He threw his arms wide open, took a deep breath and cried, "Freedom!"

95 people have died of the coronavirus in the U.S.

DAY TWO

Frank shut off the alarm. He no longer had to rise at 6:00 but he did not want to get too comfortable. This whole thing would be over in a couple of weeks, and Frank decided that he would not allow himself to get out of his routine. So, he got up when the sun was still sleeping, had a shower, dressed, and ate a quick breakfast of toast and black coffee as usual.

Normally, the commute took him an hour to get to work but he had no place to go. This left an hour to kill. He sipped on his second cup of coffee and read the news, smiling.

121 people have died of the coronavirus in the U.S.

DAY THREE

Frank decided to dress a little more casual, khakis with a light blue oxford and a tie. No jacket necessary!

After breakfast, he set up his computer on the kitchen table, neatly stacking some files he brought home from work. He looked out his bay window at his neatly trimmed yard and the birds frolicking in their birdbath.

171 people have died of the coronavirus in the U.S.

DAY SIX

Frank had no meetings today. He rolled out of bed and landed on the floor at eight-thirty-two. He smiled. He never laid on the floor before and was enjoying his newfound freedom. He could lay down on the floor anytime he wanted. Frank could not do that at the office.

He put on a pair of basketball shorts and a baggy t-shirt. He did not have a shower or eat his breakfast before sitting down at the kitchen table to work. His task today was to create a worker-productivity-during-the-first-week-of-working-remotely spreadsheet, or a WPDTFWOWR spreadsheet. He really needed to think of a better name.

Frank felt he had become more productive. No more wasted time socializing with people he did not like. No more hour-long lunches. He ate when he was hungry, not when the time said he should eat.

This is the wave of the future for many industries, Frank thought. *There may be a silver lining to this whole business, after all.*

693 people have died of the coronavirus in the U.S.

DAY TEN

Frank Smith did his work in a t-shirt and boxers. He stayed up until two in the morning, which was unusual for him. He was generally asleep by ten.

2,399 people have died of the coronavirus in the U.S.

DAY ELEVEN

Frank Smith's sleep patterns were out of whack. The more he relaxed, the less regimented he was and that started to unnerve him. He tossed and turned and paced the house instead of sleeping through the night. Now he felt a bit groggy and needed several naps during the day, but he still completed his work assignments. *No harm no foul*, he thought, *or was it no foul no harm?*

Again, Frank wore a t-shirt and boxers. He only had three pairs of boxers. Usually, he went with the classic whitey tighties, although none of them were either white or tight at this point. He spent two hours on Amazon looking at underwear. It was surprising to Frank how many pairs of underwear Amazon had! He got a pair with beer cans on them, a pair with chili peppers, and another pair with the Grinch on them for when he was in the holiday spirit.

2,825 people have died of the coronavirus in the U.S.

DAY TWELVE

This was the first day that Frank did not remember what he did. He somehow remembered he wore a t-shirt and boxers.

She had given him the t-shirt. It was dark blue with a white illustration of Spock holding up his hand in the Vulcan salutation. Above the drawing were the words, *Emotionally Unavailable*. It was one of those jokes that revealed the truth. Maybe he was emotionally stunted and that was the reason why his relationships did not last. Maybe it was just a Star Trek joke.

Regardless of the meaning of the gift, Frank Smith did not throw it away, which might have some other meaning. But meaning or not, it seemed more difficult for Frank to let it go now, when the world was unraveling. *We all need something to hold on to*, he thought.

3,251 people have died of the coronavirus in the U.S.

DAY THIRTEEN

Frank was afraid that his life was slipping away and he needed to control at least some portion of it. He made a list of what the weather was like, how much water he drank, and how much he walked. Talking to himself helped:

Walk for twenty minutes. I can walk 2,000 steps in twenty minutes. I can walk a mile in twenty-four minutes. That's two and a half miles each hour, if I were walking the whole hour, which I'm not. I'm only walking twenty minutes. But if I walked twenty minutes, ten times a day that is two hundred minutes. That's twenty thousand steps, which is eight and a half miles a day walking around my house. My little walking circle; living room, dining room, kitchen, hallway, living room, dining room, kitchen, hallway, living room, dining room, kitchen, hallway.

As Frank walked, he looked at the pictures of his family arranged in order. First were his three girls. Then Sally (his youngest) with chocolate sauce covering her face from an ice cream sundae.

Sarah (his oldest) in her first tutu at age five.

Frank and his three girls in New York.

Sandra (his middle daughter) and Sally, aged three and one respectively, looking like the terrors they were.

Lilly (his dead dog although not dead when the photo was taken).

Young Frank in a college theatrical.

Frank's parents in a gallery displaying his mother's work.

His father's parents (their wedding photo).

His mother's parents (their wedding photo).

His parents (their wedding photo).

Van Gogh (dead artist).

Harkleroad (local artist).

Birdlady (by a local dead artist).

Vincent.

MacHeath.

Life is Beautiful.

Van Gogh.

Mirror, mirror.

Frank's three girls.

Pictures on the opposite wall:

Of Mice and Men.

Whirling stairs.

Trinity Library.

Homeless Jesus.

Sarah at the big game.

Parents (aged 90).

In the kitchen, he made careful note of the magnets on the refrigerator:

- *We were all born mad, some of us remain so.*
- *Time you enjoy wasting is not wasted time.*
- *Even if the hopes you started out with are dashed, hope has to be maintained.*
- *The world is full of magic things, patiently waiting for our senses to grow sharper.*
- *Love loves to love love.*
- *Misery – It's the new happiness. At least it's attainable.*
- *Thy festering lump of nature.*
- Save the date.
- Save the date.
- Save the date.
- Save the date.
- Save the date.

And a list of groceries:

- Toilet paper
- Saline
- Coffee
- Milk

3,677 people have died of the coronavirus in the U.S.

DAY FOURTEEN

Frank no longer appreciated the novelty of the pandemic. He put on a pair of khakis and a polo, business casual.

He made a schedule for the day. It helped him focus. It helped him to not sink into despair.

- Get up.
- Wash my face.
- Morning constitutional.
- Eat my grits.
- Morning walk.
- Wash the dishes.
- Mid-morning walk.
- Mid-morning snack.
- Finish 24 ounces of water.
- Check my email.
- Late morning walk.
- Laundry.
- Early afternoon walk.
- Read.
- Midafternoon walk.
- Write my notes for the day.
- Late afternoon walk.

- Finish 48 ounces of water.
- Prepare dinner.
- Dinner.
- Early evening walk.
- Wash dishes.
- Watch a movie.
- Finish 72 ounces of water.
- After-the-movie walk.
- Read.
- Final walk of the day.
- Shower.
- Bed.

4,105 people have died of the coronavirus in the U.S.

DAY FIFTEEN

Smith wore jeans and a t-shirt. At nine a.m., he received an email stating that he would be furloughed temporarily with pay. During his second morning circle walk, he thought of survival.

Have to conserve. Have to ration. How many sheets in a roll of toilet paper? They don't have any at the store. Started on the 25th. That's ten days. Good. Four more rolls. I have forty days. Over a month. I can get more in a month. That shouldn't be difficult. But I only go to the store once a week. That's only four days. And people are hoarding. Most families have several people, a mother, a father, and two point two kids. They can cover more stores and they can hit those stores at various times. They can cover this whole area. What chance do I have against four, maybe five people? All looking for toilet paper. The stores should do something about that. The government should. It's unfair.

Smith ordered toilet paper from China on Amazon. Other items to conserve:

- Saline solution – can last a month.

- Coffee – can last two weeks.
- Milk – can last a week.
- Spinach – can last three days.
- Flour – can last a month.
- Sugar – can last six weeks.

5,770 people have died of the coronavirus in the U.S.

DAY TWENTY-ONE

S mith wrote about grits.
Grits for breakfast.
Four days this week.
Don't like to eat the same thing.
Each morning, each evening.
Like to change things up a bit,
Spice things up.
Variety is the spice of life.
Life is nothing without tedium.
No eggs, no toast, no cereal.
So, it has been grits:
   • *Cheesy grits*
   • *Cheesy spinach grits*
   • *Cheesy spinach garlic grits*
Made it four days ago.
Four to one
Four cups of water
One cup of grits
Four to one
One to four
Cook for twenty minutes.
Stir occasionally.

Could you be more precise?
No, precision is not necessary.
Throw in some garlic.
Throw in some spinach.
How much is some?
I don't know.
Do I care?
Does it matter?
Does anything matter?
Does it matter if anything matters? Not to the grits!

Turn off the heat.
Put in some cheese.
Stir, then serve.

Refrigerate the rest.
Eat the next day and the next.
Each day add a little more cheese,
A little more spinach, a little more garlic.
Add some milk.
Every day a little more.
Until there are no more (grits)
Which is what you wanted in the first place.
But not after four days.
After four days, you are tired of everything.
The circle walks.
The schedule based on tedium.
The news, which no longer feels like news,
But regurgitations of yesterday's news.

Where is the happy news?
    "I met a girl who sang the blues,
    And I asked her for some happy news."
Why would I do that?
She does not seem to be a positive person.
But who is nowadays?

Roll of toilet paper fell in the toilet.
1 roll of toilet paper in 01 day.
15,758 people have died of the coronavirus in the U.S.

DAY TWENTY-SEVEN

Frank made a playlist for his circle walks. The songs were mostly from the 60s, 70s, and 80s. He was intensely aware of how off-key he sang. Frank was not a person who sang joyfully with reckless abandon. He held back, which made the unpleasant sound more unpleasant. As an accountant, he celebrated order. His singing was neither orderly nor correct.

In T.S. Eliot's *The Confidential Clerk*, there was a character who wanted to play the organ. But as he played for other people he realized that the sound he was creating never matched the beautiful music he heard in his head. And so, he gave it up.

Frank thought that neither the clerk nor he could create beauty because neither loved themselves. *Love was necessary to move life past the mundane.*

In Frank's fifty years of life, he wondered if he loved anything. He tried, there was no doubt about that, but did he ever actually arrive at a place of joy and happiness? Frank could not be sure.

After three days of listening to music, he deleted his playlist and walked in silence, alone with his thoughts.

1 roll of toilet paper in 12 days.
29,932 people have died of the coronavirus in the U.S.

DAY THIRTY

S mith wore shorts and a t-shirt.

After lunch, he received an email from human resources.

We are sorry to inform you that because of the pandemic we are forced to let go of 20% of our employees. You are one of them. We appreciate all the loyalty you have shown Tennuteck in the past and wish you the best in the future.

Please click on the following link to apply for unemployment. https://www.usa.gov/ unemployment#item-35882

Sincerely,

blah, blah, blah

Human Resources Director

Smith looked up from his computer to his backyard. Everything was the same as it was a minute ago, but everything was different.

Tennuteck was not a bad company, although Smith, who was there for fifteen years, never knew what the company did. It did not seem important. Smith balanced books and filed reports. He filed the report that stated during a pandemic the company could function with fewer employees. He might have been responsible for getting himself fired. But that would not have stopped Smith from filing a good report.

1 roll of toilet paper in 12 days.
35,548 people have died of the coronavirus in the U.S.

DAY THIRTY-ONE

S mith could not sleep. Near his bed was a Bible. Occasionally, he would read from it, never understanding the meaning of the tales, but it helped him sleep. The book fell open to the Book of Judges and he read the story of Samson. Frank interpreted it as that a man should never trust a woman. He laughed. That would have been good advice for Smith twenty years ago. Too much trusting back then. Now he did not trust anyone. Smith wondered which holy book would help him with that.

He fell asleep before getting his answer.

The next day, he woke up still thinking of Samson. *The good thing about the Bible*, thought Smith, *was that you could say almost anything means anything, and if anyone questioned you, you could say that God came to you and told you this rhubarb. Nobody could say that God did not tell you rhubarb.*

Regardless of what God told him, this is what he thought about the whole business. Samson was stronger after he was blinded. So was Smith. *Ignorance is bliss, so is blindness to the misery of the world.*

Smith liked that expression so much he wished he could make a fortune cookie to put it in. But Smith never liked fortune cookies. He wished real cookies were fortune cookies but thought the paper would go gooey in the cookie dough. His idea needed further development. He wrote it down and stuck it on the refrigerator.

Later that day, Smith applied for unemployment.

1 roll of toilet paper in 15 days.
38,134 people have died of the coronavirus in the U.S.

FRANK SMITH

DAY THIRTY-SEVEN

Smith could no longer easily get out of bed. What was there to get up for? When he finally managed to throw some water on his face and move out of his bedroom to put on a pot of coffee, his eyes stung from the kitchen light.

It seemed as if all the lights in his house were stabbing his eyes and giving him a headache. Smith shut off the lights and spent the day doing his circle walk in the dark. From that day on, he rarely turned on any light during the day or opened the curtains.

1 roll of toilet paper in 21 days.
51,208 people died of the coronavirus in the U.S.

DAY FORTY-SEVEN

Smith tried to get his mail but his neighbor's unleashed dogs approached him, and growled viciously. Smith slowly retreated into his house and peered out the window to see if his path was clear. The dogs continued to patrol the street. After a while, Smith gave up on the notion of collecting his mail.

How many things would Smith have to deal with? Wasn't the pandemic enough? And now he was unemployed. Talking to the idiots down at the unemployment office was frustrating. He wanted to scream but he was not a person who screamed easily. Even after stubbing his toe, only a stifled *yow, yow, yow* escaped from his mouth. Too many bad things were happening, and each day life grew worse.

When the world gets scary everything becomes a conspiracy. Smith thought that the vicious hounds must be controlled by microwave beams turning them into dangerous animals. The politicians on the right and left were controlled by nefarious invisible forces. Even the Post Office was in on the plot, delivering letters willy-nilly!

Smith went into the kitchen and pulled out a roll of aluminum foil and made a helmet to protect himself from the mind-altering microwave beams used on his neighbor's dogs. The government would not take over his mind today.

He wore the hat for the rest of the day, mostly out of boredom. He could not wear it to bed, which was worrisome, because everybody knew the evil microwave beams were stronger at night.

Other conspiracies that Smith pondered:

The government taking over men's penises, thereby making them impotent. This way men would look up to strong leaders. And women would only have sex with independent penises.

Starbucks was run by a top-secret organization that put drugs in your coffee and made everybody mindless idiots.

He could not figure it out yet, but there must be some conspiracy going on behind the QWERTY keyboard. What the hell was that, anyway?

LED light bulbs emitting mind-altering photon beams. The government seemed mighty willing to get rid of incandescent light bulbs. This was another reason Frank kept all light use in his home to a minimum.

If fluoride was so good for teeth, why did he have so many cavities?

How come Myanmar, Liberia and the United States were the only three countries that had not adopted a metric system? Was Liberia or Myanmar secretly controlling the U.S. government?

Clothing manufacturers kept making their clothes smaller and smaller, so that men would think they were getting fat. That made the men more insecure, which worked in tandem with the whole government penis thing.

1 roll of toilet paper in 18 days.
65,150 people have died of the coronavirus in the U.S.

DAY FIFTY-ONE

Smith had speculated that he might have the virus. This feeling of dread had been with him for some time. Every few days he would sneeze. Once a week, he would get a headache. His throat seemed sore although he never coughed, and it did not hurt to swallow. He was having trouble sleeping.

He scheduled an appointment for that afternoon. After being weighed (he had gained two pounds sliding past 30 on the Body Mass Index and quietly into obesity) and having his blood pressure checked (it was a bit high), he told the doctor his litany of symptoms. The doctor tested Smith for Hepatitis C, Covid-19, Strep Throat, Mononucleosis, and the regular flu.

One week later, a nurse called. Everything had come back negative. Smith felt depressed and asked if he could speak with his doctor. The doctor told him to cheer up because he did not have anything but was probably stressed from what was going on in the country. The fact that the whole country was miserable did not make Smith feel any better. And now he would be embarrassed every time he came in for a check-up.

"Oh, here's Frank Smith, the biggest hypochondriac in the whole area! I hope he is happy taking up my precious time when I should be helping non-fake sick people!!!"

He could have sworn he heard the doctor laughing as he hung up the phone. Smith vowed to not return to this doctor even if he were gasping for his last breath.

1 roll of toilet paper in 25 days.

76,335 people have died of the coronavirus in the U.S.

DAY SIXTY-ONE

Smith put down his book when he heard the buzzing noise. At first, he thought it was the refrigerator's compressor again, which seemed to go off daily, but when he arrived in the kitchen, he saw a dragonfly buzzing against the overhead light. The insect was the largest he had ever seen in his house. Its wingspan must have been six inches.

Smith panicked when he saw its thousand eyes in each eye, tremendous iridescent wingspan, and tail rounded up like a scorpion's. Though in this case, its tail was rounded down because it was walking upside down on the light fixture. Frank thought dragonflies were not particularly pleasant creatures.

Smith stood frozen, afraid to move. If the creature attacked, he would be doomed. He did not like nature. His garden was overgrown. He was never able to keep pets or grow bonsai, and now Smith was facing an angry insect. Smith backed away slowly, making sure not to break eye contact. He rounded the corner and knew he was safe – unless the creature followed him into the living room.

He attempted to read and forget about the dragonfly in his kitchen. But the monster had no intention of being forgotten and continued to buzz loudly. Smith did not know what to do. Should he never go into his kitchen again? He did not need to eat as much as he was accustomed to, but some food was necessary. He would do almost anything to placate the dragonfly, but what about his circle walk? He passed right under the beast a thousand times a day. How could he do that without enraging the giant insect god?

Smith realized there was no way around this, the dragonfly must die.

He searched his garage until he found the big bottle of bug spray. He crept to the dragonfly and sprayed several quick shots at the beast, quickly retreating to the sounds of the dragonfly banging ferociously against the light. But the beast would not die. Smith screwed up his courage once again and sprayed five more times, hitting the creature directly.

The spray atomized in the air and Smith inhaled the poison as well. He dropped the sprayer as he coughed violently, fell to the ground, and waited for death to come. It didn't. He lay there, breathing heavily, until he heard a sound that made his heart rejoice. The evil beast fell to the floor, flapping its wings desperately until it flapped no more.

After another moment, Smith was able to breathe again. He stood up and saw his noble opponent lying on the kitchen floor in a puddle of insecticide. Earlier, he had thrown out an empty container of margarine. He grabbed it out of the garbage and scooped up the lifeless creature with the lid, dropped it into the tub, and tossed it back into the waste can. He hoped it would be the last creature he would need to battle in his house.

The next morning as Smith was drinking his first cup of coffee, he heard a sound. He went into the kitchen to look for what was making the noise. It was coming from under the kitchen sink. He opened the door where his garbage was located. An awful realization flowed over him, like a wave on the beach near a sewage plant. The beast he thought he killed, the creature that he inhaled half a gallon of insecticide to dispose of, was alive.

Still as angry as ever, it beat its wings in the darkness of the plastic container coating itself with the remnants of the heart-healthy butter substitute. Smith realized he could not live in the house if he let the thing stay in the garbage, so he removed the container, unlocked the back door, and popped the container lid but did not open it.

He wanted the lid to fall off as he threw it into the yard. He was never good at throwing things and the container only landed five feet away on the slab at the base of his steps. The lid fell off and the creature rolled out and sat on the ground. Smith quickly closed the door, pulling the curtain so the beast would not be able to see him with its thousand eyes. Two hours later, Smith unlocked his door and looked out. The dragonfly was gone.

Smith thought that the beast must have been some sort of immortal. Maybe a god or a fairy incapable of being killed by bug spray. Smith believed many things that people found hard to swallow. They were true just the same.

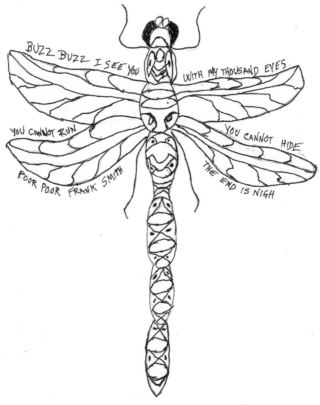

1 roll of toilet paper in 05 days.
91,380 people have died of the coronavirus in the U.S.

DAY SEVENTY-ONE

The internet said to try new things to avoid depression, get out of one's routine. The new thing Smith tried was to bake a sponge cake, which was remarkable because Smith disliked cakes.

After sixty-five minutes in the oven, the center was still like pudding. He cut away the cooked parts and threw away the goo. He did not understand his failure, but he never did. He'd followed the directions perfectly. Recipes always made it seem easier than reality.

On his next circle walk, Smith thought of God. *Religions always give us recipes for happiness although not many prophets were happy.*

Moses never got to the promised land and he was the greatest prophet of the Jews. He had one little screw-up and he was not allowed to get his reward. He could see the promised land just across the river, but he could not go there. That sounded like taunting to Smith, which was not a nice thing for an immortal to do. Jesus ended badly. Bartholomew, one of Jesus' disciples, was crucified upside down, and then because he did not die fast enough, was taken down, flayed, and beheaded.

The atheist, on the other hand, had no hope. Atheism promised nothing but death. *Well, at least you would not have to worry about being flayed,* Smith thought. *Life is what it is and then it is not.*

Happy with his conclusion, Smith continued his circle walk with no more thoughts of religious persecutions, God, or sponge cakes.

His three girls, Sally with chocolate sauce, Sarah in her tutu, Smith and the girls in New York, Sandra and Sally, Lilly, Smith in a college theatrical, parents in a gallery, father's parents, mother's parents, his parents, Van Gogh, Harkleroad, birdlady, Vincent, MacHeath, Life is Beautiful, Vincent, mirror, mirror, three girls...

1 roll of toilet paper in 19 days.

George Floyd died today in police custody. Frank hardly noticed. Another man killed in a sea of death.

Wildfires were burning in the west. Frank thought he should take note of that.

103,315 people have died of the coronavirus in the U.S.

DAY SEVENTY-THREE

Toilet paper arrived from China. Smith made a special trip to the post office. He sent the toilet paper to his postal box fearing that if it was delivered to his door, it would be stolen by marauding hordes of package thieves that seemed to be everywhere. He read about those porch pirates on the internet. The postal box was stuffed with junk mail, bills, and the key to a large locker for the toilet paper.

When he got the package home, he immediately opened it despite his many imagined concerns about postal service employees' lack of consistent healthy protocols during the pandemic. The rolls were smaller than he expected and did not have the cardboard tube in the center. They could not be put on the toilet paper holder without much effort. Smith wondered if the Chinese did that on purpose. First the virus, now this!

The paper was also light brown, reminding Smith it was supposedly made from bamboo. He wondered if this was another attempt to take over the U.S. government. Chinese Flu, no cardboard tube, brown tissue! There were too many coincidences for this to be serendipitous! Regardless of the level of serendipity, Smith vowed to use the communist toilet paper only if and when when his current supply of patriotic American toilet paper was consumed.

1 roll of toilet paper in 20 days.

2 days of social unrest in the U.S.

8,455 acres burned in wildfires in the western U.S.

105,593 people have died of the coronavirus in the U.S.

DAY NINETY-ONE

The day was cool for this time of year. It might rain later but it was a nice day to work in the yard. Get some exercise. Get some sunshine. He took his pruning shears and walked boldly into the garden, stopping before one unruly large azalea. Smith was never much of a gardener. He was a city boy who never got his hands dirty, but he liked having a yard and green things around him.

The garden was a mess. His grapevine was wilted. His fig trees produced no fruit. His olive trees had remained stunted since he planted them. When he bought his house, he thought he would be self-sufficient, living on wine, figs, and olives.

The only thing that grew were the weeds and the azaleas, rising to over eight feet in height. He walked around the monster shrub. This proved challenging. Bushes and saplings of unknown vegetation crowded the space from the back of the bush to the neighbor's fence. He cut three branches and left them on the ground, hoping to grind them up the next time he mowed the lawn.

As usual, whatever enthusiasm he had when he began quickly dissipated once he started working.

His attempts at gardening could be a metaphor for his life, full of starts and stops. He would vacuum half the house. He would leave the clean laundry in the dryer, only removing and putting it away when another load needed to be washed.

Why bother taking care of oneself? For what? For whom? There would be no dinner guests, only solitary meals watching the TV. If there were someone else in his house, a woman, he would make the effort. He always made the effort when there was a woman. But there had not been one of those in years. Maybe Smith was already on the path of reclusiveness, separating himself from his community, spurning all relationships that would make him care for others before the pandemic started. Maybe this year only sped up the journey.

You either die with someone at your side or you die alone. Either way you die. If Frank really wanted someone by his side, he would have tried harder. When he was younger, he dreamed of a large family and Sunday dinners with his loved ones filling his home with songs and laughter.

He thought he was on the right track, but he wasn't, and his marriage dissolved without much fuss. A phone call from his lawyer informed him his divorce was finalized when he was in his car, alone, coming back from a funeral.

He did not know whether he'd felt happy or sad. He felt nothing. Maybe that was the start of his separation from people, the numbness that filled his soul and clouded his mind.

The phone rang. A woman from the unemployment office called Smith for a phone interview. She asked him all sorts of questions about this and that. Smith did not pay much attention.

His mind circled back to death. He hoped he would die in his sleep. His worst fear was that he would slip in the shower, smack his head on the faucet and drown in one inch of water. People died this way; Smith read it on the internet. Then the police would find his bloated, naked corpse after a week or two. That could never look attractive. What if he was taking a shower during a thunderstorm and lightning hit the house? That was a bad one too, similar to slipping in the shower except he'd be crispy.

Smith realized there were lots of ways to die while in the shower. Home invasions also had a multitude of variables and were high on his list of worst ways to die. He made a list:

- Regular home invasions
- Large animal home invasions (bear, lion, or walrus)
- Small animal home invasions (rats, squirrels, or snakes)
- Insect home invasions (Any insect, they are all gross)

- Zombie home invasions
- Mutant home invasions
- Alien home invasions
- Zombie alien mutant home invasions

After twenty minutes, the woman from the unemployment office, still on the other end of the line, said that she knew a way to get him his money quicker. A shortcut that was not exactly the right way to proceed, but she guaranteed he would receive his money within a couple of weeks. Smith thanked her for her efforts on his behalf.

1 roll of toilet paper in 05 days.

20 days of social unrest in the U.S.

23,745 acres burned in wildfires in the western U.S.

120,534 people have died of the coronavirus in the U.S.

DAY NINETY-THREE

Two months after Smith was fired and applied for unemployment, Mr. Blanding from the office of social services called. He told Smith that his application had just been denied. Blanding said that there were shortcuts taken that led to the denial. Smith argued that whatever shortcuts were taken, it was at the recommendation of their office. The man said that Smith should not have listened to anyone from the office. If he wanted to appeal the ruling, Blanding would send the forms which should arrive in six to eight weeks.

Frank walked his circle walk. He itched his nose and then he stopped to scratch his right big toe. His left big toe seldom needed scratching as far as he could recall. The next time around his walking circle, he scratched his shoulder and his upper back, rubbing it against a wall corner. He wondered how frequently he scratched himself on his travels, so he made a list.

- Nose
- Toe
- Shoulder
- Back

- Eyebrow
- Right calf
- Left calf
- Groin
- Head
- Groin
- Head
- Groin
- Head
- Back
- Neck
- Right upper arm
- Right knee
- Groin
- Groin
- Groin
- Groin
- Head
- Left knee

It seemed that in every rotation, Frank scratched himself multiple times. He put the list on the wall and decided to take a shower. A roll of toilet paper fell into the shower.

2 rolls of toilet paper in 18 days.
22 days of social unrest in the U.S.
25,545 acres burned in wildfires in the western U.S.
121,832 people have died of the coronavirus in the U.S.

DAY NINETY-SEVEN

If he added bookshelves to the list of pictures Smith passed on his circle walk, it would read something like this: His three girls, Sally with chocolate sauce, Sarah in her tutu, Smith and the girls in New York, Sandra and Sally, Lilly, Smith in a college theatrical, parents in a gallery, father's parents, mother's parents, his parents, bookshelf #1, bookshelf #2, Van Gogh, bookshelf #3, Harkleroad, bookshelf #4, birdlady, Vincent, MacHeath, Life is Beautiful, Vincent, mirror, mirror, three girls.

Bookshelf #1 held books on loan from his sister that would probably never be returned. On other shelves, there were health books like yoga, tai chi, and various unused exercise manuals, cookbooks, and travel books.

Bookshelf #2 included plays, folk tales, history, and education. Bookshelf #3 featured works of literature, art, and architecture books. Bookshelf #4 offered more plays, biographies, and books about the performing arts.

Occasionally on his circle walks, Smith would become unfocused and bump against the wall. Today, he bumped into bookshelf #3. Two books fell with a thump. He stopped to pick up the top book, *Man in the Holocene* by Max Frisch. He remembered the story vaguely; he'd read it more than twenty years ago. An old guy in a remote village in the Alps is trapped in his house because it has been raining for weeks. Smith had been trapped in his home for ninety-six days. He could not recall how the story ended, but Smith could not imagine it ending well.

Even though this was a novel, Frisch wrote many plays. Smith debated as to where the correct place would be for this book, lonely with the novels, or with his play brothers and sisters. Smith remained lost in thought, arguing the merits of each placement until the timer rang. Because he couldn't make up his mind, he decided to find out how the book ended and placed it on a pile of to-be-read books on the coffee table.

His eyes then turned to a bound pile of pages still on the floor, *The Unpublished Poems of A. Summer*. Smith had bought it at a neighborhood yard sale. A kid in his early teens gave it to him for a quarter when he purchased a coffee mug that read, "Meh."

Smith had asked the young man who A. Summer was and how he came to possess the manuscript. The boy said it was his grandfather's. "Is it any good?" Smith had asked.

"I don't know. Never read any of his stuff."

Smith paid the quarter for the manuscript. At home, he'd put it on the shelf and forgot about it until it landed on the floor. He turned to the first page. "The Poetry of A. Summer, an unknown poet who died in obscurity."

That's a laugh, thought Smith. *Don't we all die in obscurity?*

"Canaries" by A. Summer

We are all just canaries in a coal mine
Unaware of our prison
Unaware of the invisible poisons,
seeping into our souls.
We try to sing happily,
But over the years our lungs have filled
with coal dust
We were once beautiful, once,
When our youth and passion
filled our hearts,
When we deceived ourselves into thinking
we could make a difference.

Smith thought that Mr. Summer was not very good at rhyming.

1 roll of toilet paper in 04 days.
26 days of social unrest in the U.S.
26,745 acres burned in wildfires in the western U.S.
124,734 people died of the coronavirus in the U.S.

DAY ONE HUNDRED AND ONE

Books Smith read or partially read in his incarceration during the pandemic now included:

Man in the Holocene
Krapp's Last Tape
Island of Statues
Stephen King's On Writing
No Exit
Hemingway On Writing
A Walk in the Valley
Howl
Cinderella's End
The Trial
The Good Soldier Sjeck
The Stranger
Through the Looking Glass
Fantasius Mallare
Siddhartha
The Tibetan Book of the Dead
The Holy Bible

He was pleased by the diversity of his choices, even though he hadn't finished most of them.

Frank Smith misplaced a roll of toilet paper while searching for a pair of socks.

1 roll of toilet paper in 01 day.

30 days of social unrest in the U.S.

32,645 acres burned in wildfires in the western U.S.

127,078 people have died of the coronavirus in the U.S.

BOOKCASE #1 IN MIRROR

DAY ONE HUNDRED AND TWO

Smith read a news story on the internet. People were running to get the virus. They wanted to get infected while there were still medical supplies, while there were still ventilators left. *Idiots*, thought Smith, *there are never enough supplies!*

Smith once read about people doing the same thing during the plague. He could not recall which plague, but it was one of the big ones. Something about more job opportunities if you had it and lived. So, these morons would lie down next to a corpse for the night and wake up in the morning with the plague. Frank did not know which plague, but it was not one of the small plagues.

And here we are five centuries later, Smith thought, but he did not know how many centuries later because he could not recall which plague he was thinking of. Regardless, they were doing the same thing over again. It was suicide.

Smith made a list of other ways to commit suicide.

- hanging
- shooting
- poisoning

- drowning
- falling from a great height
- being crushed by a great weight
- suffocation
- stabbing
- drug overdose

Frank once had a friend who filled a sock with quarters and walked around bad neighborhoods in the middle of the night. He was in love with someone who did not love him. (Frank knew the feeling.) His friend wanted to kill himself but was a practicing Catholic. He did not want to go to Hell, so he wanted someone else to kill him. Frank often wondered if that would work. As if there were a loophole in the suicide clause. *If you want to die and someone else kills you, then you are off the hook!*

God: "We can't touch him, Lucifer, he knew the loophole!"

Frank debated whether purposefully walking through a bad neighborhood should be added to the list, which he did just because he wanted an even ten things on his list.

In the end, he decided he could never do any of them. He did not like things around his neck, a tie or even a restrictive collar, so hanging was out. He was against firearms, so it would seem insincere to use one to end his own life. Poisoning was stupid because most people were discovered over the toilet and that was not a flattering way to be found. Plus, he would have to clean the toilet, which was not on his list of chores. Drowning was out. He had not been to the beach since watching Jaws.

Falling from a great height would be a possibility except that he was afraid of heights and did not think it was worthwhile to get over one of his phobias just to fling himself from the nearest bridge. Being crushed by a great weight seemed like something from a cartoon. Suffocation, see hanging. Stabbing would be weird to do unless you were a Roman general who just lost a battle and would fall on his sword.

Then Frank remembered that they always had some lieutenant holding the sword for him. That conversation would be awkward:

"Could you hold my sword while I fall on it?"

"You are going to fall on your sword?"

"Yes."

"Accidently?"

"Yes, no, it wouldn't be an accident if I just told you I wanted to fall on it!"

"You could have been joking."

"What?"

"Like here I am walking around, just lost the battle with the Polipoleisians. Hey, what's that sword doing there, yaahhh!"

"That is the most stupid thing I ever heard."

"Well, that's what I thought."

"It's a matter of honor!"

"Honor?"

"Yes."

"Oh, well, that's different then."

"So, you'll do it?"

"You want me to hold your sword while you fall on it?"

"Yes."

"Your sword?"

"Yes."

"Could I use my sword?"

"Why do you want to use your sword?"

"I like the hilt better."

"But mine is a better sword."

And if the lieutenant was a little like Lucy from Charlie Brown, there could also be further humiliations for the general.

Frank wanted to continue the dialogue for a bit longer but he didn't have the strength, so he went back to the list. Drug overdose. Frank had too many allergies. What if the drugs did not kill him but just made him gassy?

And walking through a bad neighborhood in the middle of the night held no appeal for Frank. He usually went to bed by ten.

Frank often dreamed of his own death. He saw himself fall off buildings and splatter. Eaten by sharks. Attacked by grizzly bears, shot, decapitated, and spontaneously combusting. He saw himself dead in his dreams but never actually died. He thought he must have a strong heart.

Unless this was a dream and he was already dead, which made any further thought of death redundant.

1 roll of toilet paper in 25 days.

31 days of social unrest in the U.S.

34,245 acres burned in wildfires in the western U.S.

127,778 people have died of the coronavirus in the U.S.

DAY ONE HUNDRED AND THREE

Frank stayed busy on the phone trying to appeal his ruling. He spent four hours on hold, pacing, waiting to speak to a human. At four hours and one minute, the phone call disconnected.

Frank's hands shook with frustration and anger. His head pounded. He could not stop pacing. He felt as if he were losing control. He raised his left hand, which began to shake. *That hand was always the weaker hand*, he thought. He raised his other hand. It shook as well.

The room started spinning and he sank to the living room rug. He debated whether he could make it to the couch. He tried. He couldn't. Frank laid down. On the bottom shelf of bookcase #4 were some DVDs. His eyes caught sight of the movie, *Falling Down*. The room went black.

1 roll of toilet paper in 19 days.

32 days of social unrest in the U.S.

34,845 acres burned in wildfires in the western U.S.

128,405 people have died of the coronavirus in the U.S.

DAY ONE HUNDRED AND SEVEN

F rank woke up and thought he was dead. The sun was shining through his window. The compressor on his refrigerator was rattling as it had been for the last month and a half. Even a slight smell of Lilly, his dog, was still there. She had died years before but somehow remained through a faint smell of wet dog that would always gladden and sadden Frank when he woke up. Lilly was there to remind him of the unconditional love he once had.

Nothing had changed from the day before. But he still thought he was dead, and he was sure he was in Hell. His day-to-day existence had all the elements of Hell: an eternity of isolation, left alone with his increasingly negative thoughts, hoping for a salvation that would never come, praying for peace.

Hope had left him as he walked endlessly in his circle walk, feeling his feet against the cold wooden floor.

He knew all the changes in the textures of the floor so well because his toes had memorized them. Little cracks by the door. Bits of food not picked up by the vacuum. Crumbs too small to see but that could be felt. This part of the rug always seemed wet, though there was no reason for it to be so.

Smith pondered as he walked. Hell seemed unnecessary. Why would you need to construct a place to torture souls when, if you just isolated people, they would torture themselves much more efficiently? No burning fire pits, no brimstone, no creatures with a taste for human flesh. Sartre said that Hell was other people. Frank thought other people were unnecessary. Each person was thoroughly capable of torturing himself.

Before turning off the lights that night, Frank stared up at his ceiling. The popcorn changed into that Hieronymus Bosch painting about Hell. All those little images of how people would be tortured after they were gone.

Did human flesh even exist after death? Of course not. Did the soul feel pain? Emotional pain maybe, but once you had left this earthly plane, your attachments to the nouns of the world evaporated. And things that you once held so dear no longer had any power over you. But, if the soul still believed it was living, then all the attachments would still exist.

Frank looked at the ceiling fan above his bed. The fan turned slowly, and dust hung from the blades. He could not remember the last time he cleaned the fan. It must have been years. If he cleaned it now, dust would fall on his bed. He could not remember the last time he washed his comforter. Probably the last time he cleaned the fan. Why would he need to wash the comforter? He hardly touched it, maybe his arms or his hands but he took a shower before bed, so they were clean.

His thoughts returned to the piece of fluff hanging from the ceiling fan blade. He should be here when it fell, he thought. Only then would he know the precise time of its descent. Why that seemed important, he could not tell. But in Hell everything was important.

Frank finished reading *No Exit*. Garcin, Inez, and Estelle ended badly, eternally.

1 roll of toilet paper in 08 days.
36 days of social unrest in the U.S.
36,235 acres burned in wildfires in the western U.S.
130,480 people have died of the coronavirus in the U.S.

DAY ONE HUNDRED AND ELEVEN

Smith found himself in the attic looking through boxes. The objects he was saving had as much a connection to his present self as his present self had to the world outside his door, no connection at all. He looked through the items with the detachment of one looking through the shelves in a dismal second-hand store. He did not recognize himself in anything. Who was that man smiling with that red-haired woman? Why was that stranger holding that child's hand?

Photo albums of false memories hidden away in a dusty attic. A metaphor for his life or was it a simile? An analogy? Words describing images. Ideas representing other ideas. Never getting any closer to the obscured truth.

"Ah! My clown suit!" he cried with great happiness.

Frank had not worn it in more than thirty years, at that Halloween party. A cardboard pumpkin on his head had completed the look. He spent the night sitting on a friend's couch not moving. When someone sat next to him, he sprang up. Usually, the unsuspecting victim spilled his drink or wet himself. Sometimes it was hard to tell. Everyone was pretty drunk.

He found clown make-up and a wig and headed downstairs with the costume. He left his boxes of memories unsealed. Let the rodents build nests in his past.

He rubbed the white makeup on his face. Frank was pale already and now he was featureless, another metaphor for his life, laughing an empty laugh as he stared judgmentally into his eyes. He took the black make-up stick and filled in his hollowed eyes, using it again for his lips.

He fitted the curly red wig to his head and thought he looked like an old Annie who had been committed to an insane asylum. "Tomorrow, tomorrow, I love you tomorrow," escaped his snarling lips.

He stepped into the white satin costume with orange stripes and zipped himself up.

Frank stood silently staring at himself in the mirror. He did not look bad. Of course, he did not look good. This was his life now. He walked into the kitchen and set the microwave timer for 22:22. He began his circle walk.

Ten minutes later, the doorbell rang. Smith opened the door.

A solar-panel salesman stood frozen, looking as if he was afraid for his life. He was accustomed to angry occupants or vicious dogs. A scary clown at two-forty-five on a July afternoon was a little more surreal.

"May I help you?" the clown said blandly.

The salesman recovered. "Um, yes! We are doing some work for one of your neighbors, and I decided to knock on a few doors and introduce myself."

"Yes?"

"Yes."

"Well, go ahead."

"What?"

"Introduce yourself."

"Yes, my name is Sam Clarkson and I'm with Southern Solar." He handed the clown his card.

Frank held the card carefully, studying it for a long time as if it held the secret to man's existence on the planet.

Sam Clarkson broke the uncomfortable silence by continuing. "Yes, well, I know your time is important so I'd like to make an appointment to come back and talk to you about how solar panels can help you."

"Solar panels can help me?" the sad clown asked hopefully.

"They are the wave of the future!"

Sam the salesman had obviously returned to his memorized sales pitch.

"You want to come back?"

"Unless right now is convenient."

As if on cue, the timer on the microwave beeped. Frank turned to go.

"Can I ask you a question?" the salesman said with more than a touch of desperation.

"What is it?" Frank said, only half turning back.

"There's a bumper sticker on your door, 'Hope is the thing with feathers.' What does that mean?"

Frank had it on his car a few years back. He sold the car but kept the sticker and put it on his front door. Why should bumper stickers only be for bumpers? It seemed a bit constricting.

The evil clown turned to the salesman who took a step back, "Hope isn't the thing with feathers?" He replied before closing the door.

Frank wore the clown costume for the rest of the day. It seemed too difficult to take off.

1 roll of toilet paper in 01 day.

40 days of social unrest in the U.S.

37,345 acres burned in wildfires in the western U.S.

132,590 people have died of the coronavirus in the U.S.

DAY ONE HUNDRED AND THIRTEEN

Two days later, Smith still had the clown costume on. The white and black of his makeup had smeared over that time, swirling into a pattern that made it hard to distinguish the features of his face.

He wanted to take the costume off but did not have the willpower to do so. He was able to turn on the shower and there he stood, bright red wig, satin white costume with orange stripes and swirls of grey, white, and black makeup running down his face. He stood in the shower for twenty minutes before he could shut off the water, unzip his costume, and stagger to the bed.

Winnie the Pooh ended badly.

1 roll of toilet paper in 22 days.
42 days of social unrest in the U.S.
38,345 acres burned in wildfires in the western U.S.
134,776 people have died of the coronavirus in the U.S.

DAY ONE HUNDRED AND EIGHTEEN

Protests spread across the country. Frank supported them from a distance. He never enjoyed getting involved. Nothing against the protesting, he just wasn't a protestor. He went online and ordered a BLM silicone wristband.

Frank was right, *Man in the Holocene* ended badly.

1 roll of toilet paper in 05 days.

47 days of social unrest in the U.S.

68,345 acres burned in wildfires in the western U.S.

137,751 people have died of the coronavirus in the U.S.

DAY ONE HUNDRED TWENTY-THREE

Smith greeted the morning full of energy. He wanted to do something important today, something meaningful, but could not remember what. He woke in the night with a great idea, one of those ideas that in Smith's mind could change humanity. Usually, he would write the idea down or send it to himself in a text. He did neither last night, thinking that the idea was too good to be forgotten.

Too bad for humanity. He forgot.

He was consumed with the idea of remembering during his first circle walk. He rubbed his temples and scrunched up his face, demanding recollection. *But memories are fickle fairies flittering in the edges of our vision,* Smith thought. *If we turn our heads, they disappear.* Love is a rose, but you better not pick it, and so on and so forth.

In the end, he settled himself down in his TV chair and watched three episodes of Monk. When he slid out of the chair to break the spell of the TV, he crawled to the middle of his living room and took a nap on the rug that still smelled like Lilly. She liked that part of the rug, preferring it to sitting on Smith's lap. That was just the kind of dog she was.

After an hour, he had no desire to achieve anything. *The world does not need my help to change,* he thought. It did fine without him before he was around and would be fine after he was gone. His insignificant contribution would change nothing. Besides, after a circle walk, three episodes of Monk, and a rug nap, there was nothing that Smith wanted to change.

He remembered after his father retired, the old man's inability to accomplish anything, to do anything without hours of preparation. Even to leave the house for a walk could not be accomplished until a hundred tiny rituals were performed like some elaborate religious ceremony where any misstep was sure to enrage the gods. And the gods were not to be enraged as one walked across the street in the attempt to buy a periodical or to achieve some other equally important task.

Smith now understood his father, what he went through. He was becoming his father. If truth be told, he was always his father but only now realized it. *That is humanity's curse, we are our parents. Just another reason to hate oneself.*

1 roll of toilet paper in 12 days.

52 days of social unrest in the U.S.

70,345 acres burned in wildfires in the western U.S.

141,530 people have died of the coronavirus in the U.S.

DAY ONE HUNDRED THIRTY-THREE

Frank thought of Noam Chomsky, as he often did. He had never read Noam Chomsky but knew that Chomsky was a great modern philosopher. Noam Chomsky thought the two greatest existential problems facing mankind were nuclear war and climate change.

Frank did not understand the threat of nuclear war. In a world where resources were shrinking, it would seem wise to conserve and work together to ensure all people were taken care of. But the U.S., Russia, and China were in a contest to see who could push whom around more to the detriment of all. These great leaders wanted to show the world who had the biggest penis. North Korea would have liked to get into the contest as well, but everyone knew its leader had a very small penis.

Frank searched the internet for how far he was from the nearest military installation. Fifteen miles. Which would mean if Russia exploded a 110-megaton bomb, he would be in a moderate blast damage radius. At 5 psi overpressure, most residential buildings collapsed, injuries were universal, fatalities would be widespread. The chances of a fire starting in a damaged building were high, and damaged structures were also at high risk of spreading fires. This was often used as a benchmark for moderate damage in cities. Optimal height of burst to maximize this effect was 14.5 kilometers. In other words, Frank probably would not survive the blast, but if he did, his house would be destroyed. That was a shame, because he only had three years left on his mortgage.

If Russia was frugal and only released a 50-megaton bomb, he would do better. At around 1 psi overpressure, glass windows could be expected to break. This could cause many injuries in people who approached a window after seeing the flash of a nuclear explosion (which traveled faster than the pressure wave). This was often used as a benchmark for light damage in cities. Optimal height of burst to maximize this effect was 17.2 kilometers.

Frank hoped that it was China who would destroy everyone. They would most likely set off a 5-megaton bomb. Third degree burns extended throughout the layers of skin and were often painless because the burns destroyed the nerves. They could also cause severe scarring or disablement and often required amputation. 100% probability for third degree burns. For the people who survived within this radius, they would be walking around with flesh melting from their faces. Luckily, because there were so many gun owners in the area, the victims would be quickly put out of their misery.

The rich would hunker down in bunkers while the average person would burn above. The atmosphere would not be safe for a few generations. The survivors would spawn thousands of inbred offspring who were no better than their ancestors at caring about others, and so the madness would continue. Frank thought it might be better to go quickly.

But Frank knew the apocalypse would not come from nuclear bombs falling from the sky. It would arrive in a gradual, almost imperceptible manner as the bonds between people faded, and they no longer cared about their neighbors, their community, their country, or any of the people with whom they shared the planet. Death wouldn't come from above; it would come from within.

Frank's Black Lives Matter wristband arrived. He would never wear it outside, too controversial. But he wore it inside to support equal justice under the law.

Frank thought *Howl* ended badly, although he could not be sure.

1 roll of toilet paper 09 days.

62 days of social unrest in the U.S.

336,145 acres burned in wildfires in the western U.S.

150,509 people had died of the coronavirus in the U.S.

DAY ONE HUNDRED THIRTY-EIGHT

Smith went to get the mail, his daily ritual regardless of what day it was. Even on Sunday, he walked out front and looked both ways before opening the mailbox. He thought maybe a neighbor would think he was so busy that he could not pick up his mail the day before. What could he have done on Saturday to keep himself so preoccupied? *Yes,* thought Smith, everyone would think he was very important if they only peeked out their window and saw their neighbor checking his mail on Sunday!

Regardless of what the neighbors thought, the trip to the mailbox allowed him to go outside for a minute or two, a privilege that he'd mostly denied himself. He did not walk around his quiet, safe neighborhood. He rarely worked in his garden or mowed his lawn. He just kept walking his circle walk, thinking his circular thoughts.

But now he was ready to go outside and get his mail.

Smith opened the door and he noticed something from the corner of his eye. It looked like a small black snake. He knew it could not be a small black snake, but he thought it anyway. He must have been dreaming. But as he returned from the mailbox (empty-handed), he saw a black lizard with yellow lines and a blue tail crawling on his wall above the Birdlady. It was not a dream. It was a skink! Smith did not like lizards or any creatures in his house and although the skink was not poisonous, it did have a painful bite.

He picked up a broom and tried to whack it, hitting the painting of the Birdlady by mistake, and knocking it to the ground. The skink jumped to the floor as Smith followed, swinging the broom wildly, knocking over candles and old discarded flower pots that Smith had meant to put in the garage but never got around to doing. He never got around to anything.

The creature scurried into the kitchen and under the oven. Now the little bugger had sanctuary and Smith would stay up nights thinking it would attack him. It was a battle of man versus beast or man versus nature. Whatever the nature of this epic conflict, Smith was bound to lose.

The slithering skink was not seen the next day, or the day after or the day after that. Almost two months would pass before the confrontation with the beast would be unhappily concluded.

1 roll of toilet paper in 07 days.

67 days of social unrest in the U.S.

371,145 acres burned in wildfires in the western U.S.

157,145 people have died of the coronavirus in the U.S.

DAY ONE HUNDRED THIRTY-NINE

S mith took the save-the-date postcards off the re-frigerator. Dates no longer needed to be saved.

No joyful family gatherings. No mournful family gatherings designed for loved ones to comfort each other in sorrow and loss.

1 roll of toilet paper in 22 days.

42 days of social unrest in the U.S.

38,345 acres burned in wildfires in the western U.S.

134,776 people have died of the coronavirus in the U.S.

DAY ONE HUNDRED FIFTY-THREE

S mith wondered how he got to this place. Not his physical place although there were times when he wondered about that as well. He wondered about his emotional place. That he was isolating in isolation. In all his life, there was no one whom he cared for enough, that cared enough for him, that together they would be able to struggle through this solitude.

Certainly there were times when he thought he'd loved one woman enough that she could break his heart. He'd stood on the edge of a cliff, staring at the cold waters below, wondering how long his suffering would continue if he took another step. Would his heart give out when it understood that death was forthcoming?

Or would he survive the fall only to be broken by the boulders beneath the foamy tide? Or would he just be battered enough by the descent to drown unconscious in the cold, gray waters? Or would his broken body be carried off by the tide as he feebly tried to rescue himself?

His ex drove him to the edge but wasn't kind enough to finish the job. It was much more amusing to leave him there because she knew he wasn't strong enough to take the final step.

The opposite was just as true. There were other times when Frank would wake in the night wondering who the person was beside him. He knew her because they had been together for years, but her breathing offended him. He knew he could not, would not commit to their relationship because eventually she would hurt him.

There must have been moments of happiness in his life but the very acknowledgement of the joy made Smith aware that the relationship was in reality, over, like a patient in hospice care. The end was clear.

As the great unpublished poet, A. Summer, wrote:

> *I used to want a woman beside me*
> *To wake me up with a gentle kiss.*
> *I don't know what I want anymore.*
> *Although, a kiss would be nice.*

After thinking a while, Smith concluded that middle school was the reason he was in this place. Three reasons, really.

Number One. Forensics Club. Which was not the cool science of detecting crime, but the lame poetry reading club. Smith tried out for his middle school team. He thought he did well, but he did not make the team. He was so upset; he went to the coach. She told him, "You did well, but I didn't want you to make a fool of yourself."

A deflated eleven-year-old Frank couldn't help but think: *If I would have made a fool of myself in something I'm good at, then what chance do I have in the things I'm bad at?*

Number Two. They used to make kids climb ropes in gym class. The goal was to touch a red ball at the very top. They shimmied up and then shimmied down. Simple. Little Frankie found himself three feet from the ceiling but could not complete his journey. The whole class and the gym teacher taunted him to go on, but he could not do it. He stared at the red ball, knew he could touch it if he just reached out, but he froze, unable to touch the ball.

After five minutes, he slid down, forever a rope climbing failure.

Number Three. Frankie had a crush on Betty in the 7th grade. They were good friends. But Betty was seeing Johnny, Frankie's best friend. Then Johnny broke up with Betty and Betty called Frankie on the phone.

"Who will you go out with next?" Frankie joked.

"You," Betty responded.

Frankie was so flustered he made an excuse to get off the phone. Betty never asked again. When Frankie summoned the courage to ask her out, she was seeing someone else. After that, they drifted apart.

In college, Smith took a psychology course. The professor described a condition known as a fear of success. As if struck by lightning, he realized that in all three instances from middle school, he was afraid of the consequences of success.

Smith thought about those three moments in his circle walk. He was never happy in activities he chose to do. Always giving just enough but not actually trying to succeed. After all, if he didn't try, he'd never fail.

Frank's avoid-failure philosophy permeated his professional life. He went from job to job, just doing what was easiest to do, never concerned about climbing the corporate ladder. After fifteen years at Tennuteck, he was still lower middle management. Never a shooting star. Easy to forget. Easy to let go.

What if I'd said "okay" on the phone that day? Would I be happy now? Would Betty? He'd looked her up on the internet; she was a dog groomer who made house calls on Long Island.

In his personal life, he had two kinds of relationships. The first type was where the woman loved him, and he pushed her away. If he made a real commitment and it didn't work out, that would be terrible, so he didn't.

The second type was where he hung on too long, even after she lost all interest. He supposed he couldn't lose if she never really cared, or so he rationalized. Either way, he might as well have been in love with a squirrel.

There were so many moments in his life that sent Smith off in the wrong direction and once he was on that path he could not go back. *Those bastards say, today is the first day of the rest of your life, like every day could be a new beginning,* thought Smith. *I can't go back. I can only go forward and the road has led me here.*

"Just take the step. Just say okay. Just touch the damn ball," Smith said under his breath. He could have screamed it. No one was listening, not even himself.

1 roll of toilet paper in 20 days.

82 days of social unrest in the U.S.

423,178 acres burned in wildfires in the western U.S.

173,157 people have died of the coronavirus in the U.S.

DAY ONE HUNDRED SIXTY

Frank came upon another poem by A. Summer and began to wonder if he'd known A. Summer in another life. Frank had read that could happen.

"Desperation"

desperation fills you
drop by drop
grain by grain
until there is nothing left
of what you were.
You now call
the desperation
by your name.

1 roll of toilet paper in 05 days.

89 days of social unrest in the U.S.

3,067,459 acres burned in wildfires in the western U.S.

180,604 people have died of the coronavirus in the U.S.

DAY ONE HUNDRED EIGHTY-ONE

Schools were opening. Stupid schools. Smith remembered when he went to school, the teachers would always ask what he did during his summer vacation. Smith would always make up something ridiculous, something unbelievable to cover up that he never went anywhere. His family was too poor. This year he would not have had to make up anything ridiculous. He walked in his circle walk ten miles a day, a thousand cycles. He decided to video himself on his walk.

He tried to keep his phone steady, but he failed miserably. He went around three times in about a minute. He stopped recording and he looked at the video on his phone. Smith realized that he needed multiple angles. He recorded his walk holding the camera by his knees and then over his head. He recorded his walk while focusing on his face. His final video was taken looking from his belly up. Smith thought he looked like a turtle with its neck out.

After an exhausting five minutes of recording his circle walk, he reviewed his work. Smith watched the video as he walked in his circle. The screen was at eye level. His walking and the recordings did not match. When he was in the hall the video was showing him walking in his kitchen, which was disorienting. This viewing/walking business did not last long before he slammed his foot into the coffee table.

With a loud crack he fell to the floor holding his foot in pain, but the video continued to walk. Smith's brief and unpleasant voyage into independent filmmaking ended.

1 roll of toilet paper in 04 days.

110 days of social unrest in the U.S.

3,922,019 acres burned in wildfires in the western U.S.

199,000 people have died of the coronavirus in the U.S.

DAY ONE HUNDRED EIGHTY-THREE

Smith had not called anyone in the last three months. He was tired of the same conversations.

"Trump good."

"Trump bad."

"Trump good!"

"Trump bad!"

"Trump GOOD!"

"Trump BAD!"

"TRUMP GOOD!"

"TRUMP BAD!"

"Covid fake."

"Covid real."

"Covid fake!"

"Covid real!"

"Covid FAKE!"

"Covid REAL!"

"COVID FAKE!"

"COVID REAL!"

There were two known variants of this conversation because people of different minds were no longer able to have a civil conversation with one another.

Variant #1

"Trump good."

"Trump good!"

"Trump GOOD!"

"TRUMP GOOD!"

"Covid fake."

"Covid fake!"

"Covid FAKE!"

"COVID FAKE!"

"A child from the next town over was abducted by a pizza eating socialist pedophile because they drink the blood of Christian virgins!"

"I heard that too!"

"Lou Dobbs."

"Lou Dobbs."

"Lou Dobbs."

"Lou Dobbs."

Variant #2 went something like this:

"Trump bad."

"Trump bad!"

"Trump BAD!"

"TRUMP BAD!"

"Covid real."

"Covid real!"

"Covid REAL!"

"COVID REAL!"

"Everyone everywhere has died of Covid!"

"I heard that too!"

"Rachel Maddow."

"Rachel Maddow."

"Rachel Maddow."

"Rachel Maddow."

If the conversation continued into the next stage, it drifted away from the pandemic and politics, but not in any meaningful way:

"So, how are you doing?"

"Fine, fine, and you?"

"The same. Anything new?"

"No, and you?"

"No. Any new projects?"

"Yesterday I counted the light bulbs in my house."

"Cool. How many?"

"How many what?"

"Light bulbs?"

"Sorry, I just thought of something."

"What was it?"

"What was I thinking? I forgot."

This desperate babble would go on for another ten minutes before either party could think of a reason to get off the line. After all, there were no ready reasons. Nowhere to go. Nothing to do.

Smith read an article once about the need to stay connected with people, with one's tribe, to keep positive in isolation. It seemed that connecting did nothing for him except to highlight how terrible his life was. He was so lonely that superficial connections became unbearable.

He felt the same disconnection with his children. They were grown. They were gone. They had their own lives which, for the most part, did not include him. He did not blame them. He didn't.

A postcard every once in a while would have been nice, although he hadn't sent any himself. Postcards. Stamps. Letterboxes. Did they even exist anymore? Still, to receive a postcard would have been nice. To let him know that he was thought about. That he was remembered. Would he feel different being remembered? He'd enjoy a glimpse from somewhere else. A beach. A waterfall. A skyline. Somewhere exotic. Somewhere exciting. Other than here. Other than now.

Smith thought that he was lucky not to be in a relationship right now. Having to think about another person. Having to care about any other person's problems. He could barely get through the day dealing with his own issues.

Relationships are fragile things, he thought on lap 257 of his circle walk. Even incidental events could end a relationship abruptly. Smith thought of all his past relationships and how they ended because of his stupidity. He wrote a partial list:

- Laughing at inappropriate times, for example, at a funeral.
- Farting at inappropriate times, for example, at a funeral.

- Burping at inappropriate times, for example, at a funeral.

Smith recalled inappropriate behavior during at least five funerals leading to the end of various relationships. He went to many funerals.

He once sneezed in a woman's bowl of soup on the first date. They did not have a second date. He concluded that all activities that sent bodily fluids into the troposphere should be avoided.

Other relationship ending behaviors:

- Speaking up.
- Not speaking up.
- Waffling between speaking and not speaking up.
- Not answering a direct question.
- Not answering an indirect question.
- Answering a direct question.
- Answering an indirect question.
- Answering a direct question indirectly.
- Answering an indirect question directly.
- Using analogies.
- Using metaphors.
- Using parables.

Most figures of speech could lead to trouble, especially irony, alliteration, puns, and oxymorons. Maybe this was why so many poets were depressed.

After many years of fruitless relationships, Frank realized it was best to remain quiet, to smile kindly, while reducing all bodily functions to a minimum.

At least he could walk on his circle walks without fear of condemnation.

1 roll of toilet paper in 06 days.

114 days of social unrest in the U.S.

3,926,019 acres burned in wildfires in the western U.S.

203,167 people have died of the coronavirus in the U.S.

DAY ONE HUNDRED EIGHTY-SEVEN

Smith began to dread the nights. The days were filled with exhausting tedium, but the darkness had its own terrors.

If he woke up, and he always woke up, he would go to the bathroom, take a drink of water, and return to bed where he would not be able to fall back asleep. He had no thoughts to trouble his mind, but his body would not let him drift off. His bad back or his frozen shoulder or the thousand other pains that came with age flared up to remind him of his mortality.

He tried numerous positions, at first for 30 to 40 seconds, but gradually decreasing the time between adjustments until he was slashing and thrashing in the bed. Then his breathing would stop. In that moment, his body would stop as well. He could not breathe, not because it wasn't possible to breathe, but because he had forgotten how to breathe.

So, he lay there, unable to breathe, caught in a frozen moment of panic. Suddenly, there would come a great gasp and his lungs would fill with air. Just as suddenly, he pushed out the breath. Then the frozen panic came again. He was so afraid that if he did not stay awake and force himself to breathe, he would die of suffocation in bed.

His panic lasted for over an hour, until he was so exhausted, he slipped into unconsciousness. Sometimes, this sleep would last for the rest of the night. Other times he would wake an hour or two later and repeat the same torturous game.

1 roll of toilet paper in 15 days.

116 days of social unrest in the U.S.

3,930,019 acres burned in wildfires in the western U.S.

204,114 people have died of the coronavirus in the U.S.

DAY ONE HUNDRED EIGHTY-NINE

Smith made a list of things he did not like: Turkey because it was big and tasted like chicken.

Chicken because everything tasted like it.

Movies from the 70s.

Empty peanut butter jars. Should he be holding on to them for storage? How many jars could he possibly use? And to store what?

Junk mail. Why did he have to get any mail? *Postcards would be nice.* What was the purpose of most mail anyway now that everyone had email?

Junk email. Once Smith clicked on an advertisement for African clothing in a distracted moment, and now he got pop-up ads all the time. For some reason, the computer thought he was a woman and sent him advertisements to help him with his lady problems.

Socks with holes in them. He had a container with holey socks that he believed he would darn one day, but he never would.

The word darn.

The word walrus. He always had trouble with saying that word when he was younger.

Walruses. Because they looked like his Uncle Max.

His uncle Max, who used to sell buttons. He would always tell Smith how much his shoes cost.

Old shoes. Smith never knew when to throw a pair away, so he had a pile of 300 shoes in his closet.

His closet with 300 shoes in it. There were too many shoes. He couldn't put anything else in there.

Closets in general. They were dark places where things got lost.

Getting lost in dark places. Usually in big cities, where nobody would help.

Big cities. The pace was way too frenetic and unforgiving.

Unforgiving people who desired forgiveness.

Forgiving people, who never let go of their anger.

The pain he still felt from love that left him.

Women no longer in his life.

Women.

Smith feared women. How they made him feel that he was never good enough. How they demanded his honesty, but kept their truths hidden. He hated the loneliness that he felt. But he was afraid to open himself to heartache again.

The dull continuing pain of loneliness was preferable to the stabbing pain of a broken heart. They wanted Frank to change. They wanted him to wash the dishes. They wanted him to mow the lawn. They wanted him to take down his pictures and change his furniture.

And after they made their mark, they left him, with his new uncomfortable furniture, and his complementary colored walls...and his broken heart.

1 roll of toilet paper in 15 days.
118 days of social unrest in the U.S.
3,948,219 acres burned in wildfires in the western U.S.
206,014 people have died of the coronavirus in the U.S.

DAY ONE HUNDRED NINETY-ONE

Fifty-three days after the skink ran under the stove, Smith saw the monster again. Smith was vacuuming the other half of the house and moved his TV chair. There lay a non-slithering skink, shriveled up like a long black raisin, its blue neon tail no longer bright, no longer neon.

Smith felt uneasy joy as the creature was sucked up into the whirling vacuum. He watched as pieces of it bounced against the clear, plastic cup. *If we could only forget our troubles until they shrivel up from lack of attention,* Smith thought. *Usually, we are too busy encouraging our problems, enabling them to grow unimpeded.*

But Smith was not done with the beast because it came to him in a dream.

"Why are you hiding from your life, Smith? I was once like you, finding sanctuary beneath the warm oven. But my life passed in an illusion of safety. Are any of us ever safe? Look at the world, Smith. I would rather have been out in the wild fields with birds flying overhead looking to gobble me up or hiding from raccoons, snakes, and other toothy, clawing creatures than to have died in the safety of the stove. You are in a stove, Smith. You walk around it a thousand times, but you are not safe. Your world is collapsing, and you are being crushed. If you can breathe, there is no safety. If you can see, there is always desire. If you can feel, there is always heartbreak. But you must live in spite of it all."

1 roll of toilet paper in 12 days.

120 days of social unrest in the U.S.

3,955,019 acres burned in wildfires in the western U.S.

207,549 people have died of the coronavirus in the U.S.

DAY ONE HUNDRED NINETY-SEVEN

The weather report stated that there were several systems forming in the Atlantic. Smith always took hurricanes seriously, and this season was going to be an active one. He usually left the area when a storm approached, visiting friends further inland. This year, he had no place to go. Because of the virus, all doors were closed to him.

When one of the tropical storms was given the name of Millicent, Smith thought he was in trouble. His third-grade teacher was named Millicent Dixon and she hated Smith for reasons unknown to him. It was a year of hell, one of many.

Then the forecasters predicted the storm would hit his area. Smith went to his garage, took out his pre-cut boards and nailed them into place. He could never get the ladder to sit just right. It rocked with every rung he climbed, so he tried to stay as close to the ground as possible. This caused him to stretch beyond what he could do comfortably. For days after, his arms were sore.

Boarding the windows took most of the morning, leaving him sweaty, and achy, and covered with mosquito bites. Mosquitos always seemed most vicious before a storm.

He sat panting on a kitchen chair. After two glasses of water, the sweating had not stopped. He decided to take a shower, which only exhausted him more. Smith fell onto his bed dripping wet, not having the desire to towel himself off.

1 roll of toilet paper 19 days.

126 days of social unrest in the U.S.

4,055,019 acres burned in wildfires in the western U.S.

212,141 people have died of the coronavirus in the U.S.

DAY TWO HUNDRED AND ONE

Smith made a list of all the TV shows and movies he'd watched in isolation during the pandemic:

- *Harry Potter* - All
- *Diehard* – All
- *Bourne* – All
- *Lord of the Rings* – All
- *Monk* – All
- *Cougartown* – All
- *Bones* – All
- *Life in Pieces* – All
- *Parks and Recreation* – All
- *The Simpsons* – First twelve seasons
- *Hamish Macbeth* – All
- *Peter Pan*
- *Winnie the Pooh* – Twice
- *Music and Lyrics*
- *About a Boy*
- *Notting Hill*
- *Love, Actually*
- *A Clockwork Orange*
- *Citizen Kane*
- *Rebel Without a Cause*

- *Star Wars* - First three movies (Or was it the second three?)
- *The Godfather* - All
- *Midnight Run*

Frank looked at the list. If he removed all the TV shows that he stumbled upon over the last two hundred and one days –and two of the movies– the remaining list consisted of things he'd watched with his children before they were teenagers, before his marriage dissolved. He was a good father then. He was a better father than a husband. Maybe that was the problem. In the divorce, the children went with their mother. After fifteen years of marriage, he was alone.

Frank looked at the pictures of his children on the walls. His three girls, Sally with chocolate sauce, Sarah in her tutu, Smith and the girls in New York, Sandra and Sally. As he walked his circle-walk, he always looked at the pictures of when his girls were very young. If time could only have stopped then, Frank would have died a happy man. Of course his kids would have been devastated.

Now their world did not revolve around him anymore and if he died, they would be less devastated. This made Frank happy until he thought about how much he missed them and then he became sad. The world reached equilibrium again.

Maybe he would call one of them today. But he didn't want to interfere with their lives. They were busy. They were happy. What right did he have to impose? *Cat's in the Cradle* and all that. Still, maybe he would call today. Maybe tomorrow. Yes, tomorrow would probably be better.

1 roll of toilet paper in 20 days.

134 days of social unrest in the U.S.

4,055,019 acres burned in wildfires in the western U.S.

215,028 people have died of the coronavirus in the U.S.

DAY TWO HUNDRED AND TWO

The busy hurricane season had not, so far, sent a storm in Smith's direction. A week ago, Millicent was little more than a tropical wave. Now it was expected to make landfall as a category one hurricane.

He put the kettle on to make some coffee. The internet predicted Millicent would arrive by six that night. He looked at the clock on the wall. Only ten more hours to go.

Frank could do nothing but wait. On his first circle walk of the day, he decided on a breakfast of cheesy, garlic grits. He killed an hour by the time he made them, ate them, and cleaned up the kitchen.

He opened his door. The sky was overcast. He walked down the block. His neighbors were not busily preparing for the hurricane. It looked like any other day on his street. Fred, Frank's neighbor from across the street, was mowing his lawn.

He used to talk to Fred occasionally, when they crossed paths picking up their mail. He was a nice guy, an insurance salesman. Two years ago, he married a woman. Then he lost thirty pounds. Then he renovated his entire home. Must have cost a fortune. Then Fred built a pagoda looking thing in his backyard. Then he planted a garden. He did not do anything before she married him. She made him comb his hair and shave, even on the weekend. *What a sucker*, thought Frank.

Frank walked down the street smiling to himself. Another man was mowing his grass. A woman was weeding her flowerbeds.

"Are you going to evacuate?" Smith asked.

Old Mrs. Mulvaney turned from her hibiscus. "Oh, no dear. My car won't go much further than the Piggly Wiggly and back."

"Are you worried?"

"I've lived through some pretty big storms. If God wanted to take me, he would have done so already. Now these hibiscuses might have a tough time of it," she said, turning back to her flowers.

Frank returned home, looking at the boarded-up windows. "The neighbors probably think I'm a frightened baby," he mumbled as he locked the door. "I don't care what they think, and I don't want those damned hibiscus flowers ruining my lawn when this is all over!"

Smith had not mowed his lawn in over a month. A few hibiscus flowers might brighten up the place.

He had another cup of coffee, adding some Kahlua to it. His next cup, he added equal amounts of coffee and Kahlua. His third cup, he added a few drops of coffee to his Kahlua. When it was time for his second circle-walk, he took the almost empty bottle of liquor with him. Smith did not recall how long he walked but he knew he didn't cover much distance. The kitchen timer beeped to signal the end of his walk and he collapsed on the living room rug and slept for hours.

When Frank regained consciousness, he was drenched in sweat. His head felt like it was about to explode. Stumbling into the bedroom, he stripped naked and put on a clean pair of boxers and a white undershirt. He looked in the mirror and his arms were bruised from bumping into the walls as he'd staggered about.

Then he noticed the wind was howling. The time was 5:45. Millicent had arrived.

He needed a bit of the hair of the dog that bit him. Searching the liquor cabinet, he grimaced realizing he had finished the Kahlua. An old bottle of brandy sat alone on the shelf. The horrible beverage was given to him at a dinner party years ago. He hated brandy and thought that the person who gave it to him must have also hated it. That's why Smith got it. "Beggars can't be choosers," he sighed.

He twisted off the lid and took a long slug, spitting out most of it because of the vile taste. But he was a man, damn it, and he *was* going to be drunk during the storm. He took a smaller sip, followed by several more. *Brandy did not taste bad after you got four or five ounces down you,* he thought. By the time the bottle was half gone, Frank was all gone.

1 roll of toilet paper in 08 days.

131 days of social unrest in the U.S.

4,056,019 acres burned in wildfires in the western U.S.

215,455 people have died of the coronavirus in the U.S.

DAY TWO HUNDRED AND THREE

Frank woke up under the bed the next morning. He realized he was under his bed when he sat up and smacked his head on the underside of the bed. When Frank woke up the second time an hour later, he managed to crawl out without hurting himself.

The power was off and would likely not be restored until later that day. Frank walked around his house, still in his boxers and t-shirt. All-in-all the inside of his house came out all right. He put on his Crocs and stepped into his backyard. The ground was saturated. He lost his left Croc in the mud. Trying to compensate for the Croc-sucking suction of the mud, he fell backwards, landing on the wet ground and losing his second shoe. Frank struggled to get upright and then collected both shoes. He washed his muddied feet and shoes off with the garden hose. The gush of water had a rhythm. Frank hummed a song as he looked around the yard.

> *What's the use of worrying?*
> *It never was worthwhile*
> *So, pack up your troubles in your old kit bag,*
> *And smile, smile, smile.*

His smile turned into a sneer when he saw it. He hated that one tree. He hated it as much as any man could hate a tree. The oak was not a bad tree as far as oaks go, but it was leaning at a disturbing angle. This was not due to Millicent. The tree had been leaning when Frank bought the house.

He used to think it had a certain charm. Then he thought it was quirky. Now he just hated it and plotted many ways to get rid of it. He could have called a landscaper to cut it down, but he always got distracted. *One day you just wait, one day*, he threatened the tree.

> *So, pack up your troubles in your old kit bag,*
> *And smile, smile, smile.*

He looked over and saw his neighbor's thirteen-year-old daughter staring at him, horrified. His back, turned from her with the running hose held at waist height, created a disturbing image. To complete the look, his mud-stained boxers and tee shirt would probably be responsible for years of therapy for the young girl.

He held up the garden hose in one hand and raised the other in a sort of lame wave, but she'd already turned to run away from the sight of him. Frank went back inside and slammed the door. *Nosy neighbors, why couldn't they mind their business and keep their prying eyes in their own yards?*

He had cold leftover cheesy, garlic grits for breakfast and poured the rest of the brandy down the drain.

Later, with the power still out and little to do, Frank threw a roll of toilet paper at a squirrel.

2 rolls of toilet paper in 05 days.

132 days of social unrest in the U.S.

4,057,019 acres burned in wildfires in the western U.S.

216,265 people have died of the coronavirus in the U.S.

DAY TWO HUNDRED AND TEN

Seven days after Millicent barreled through town, Hurricane Ophelia arrived. Frank did not bother taking down the window boards from the last hurricane, so he had some extra time to prepare. He used it well by going to the liquor store to buy rum and Cointreau Next, he headed to the Bi-Lo to get some lime juice. Cuban Sidecars were on the menu for tonight.

Ophelia was set to make her debut as a Category 3 hurricane somewhere around three in the morning. *Why do they always seem to arrive in the middle of the night?* Frank wondered.

By eleven, Frank was plastered. He had been on his circle walk for the last two hours with a forty-ounce Tervis container filled to the brim with his Caribbean refresher. His condition allowed him to imagine himself as a great Shakespearean actor shouting lines to his adoring fans. "Blow, winds, and crack your cheeks! rage! blow! You cataracts and hurricanoes, spout...'Til you have drench'd our steeples, drown'd the cocks!"

"Ha! Cocks!" he babbled almost incomprehensibly. "Shakespeare could write cocks and get away with it.

That man could write anything, and people loved it. Why are some people just lucky that way?"

He pondered this as the rain pelted his house. The noise was so loud that Smith had to put down his drink to place his hands over his ears. This only amplified the weather more.

He staggered around his house looking like a drunken elephant as he continued his recitation. "Drowned cocks...steeples...for in that sleep of death what cheeks may come tomorrow, and tomorrow, and tomorrow. If you prick us–he said prick–are we not full of sound and fury, signifying nothing. Is this a Tervis I see before me?"

Frank had rounded the kitchen again and saw his drink standing lonely on the floor. He knelt to retrieve his libation. A flash of lighting, a crack of thunder and the lights went out. Frank flattened himself on the floor.

When he thought the coast was clear, he crawled the rest of the way to his bottle. Hugging the flask as if it were an old friend, he took a long slug and said, "We have seen better days."

Frank passed out in the hallway.

He sat up five hours later not sure where he was. The wind rushing around his house sounded like a freight train. Then he heard a large crack. The whole house shook as the tilting oak tree from Frank's yard came crashing through the roof above his bedroom, a large limb piercing his bed. Had he been sleeping, he would have met a quick, peaceful, and somewhat gruesome death.

But he was sitting up in the hallway at the time. The power was off. The night was dark and noisy with a cold, wet wind blowing across his face through Frank's newly opened roof.

He walked to the bedroom door and looked at the branch piercing his bed, the rain pouring through the hole in the roof, pictures and clothes scattered on the floor. He sighed, took a step back, and closed the bedroom door. Frank shuffled off to the living room to sleep on the couch. All the destruction would be there in the morning. He would deal with it then.

1 roll of toilet paper in 23 days.

139 days of social unrest in the U.S.

4,063,019 acres burned in wildfires in the western U.S.

221,307 people have died of the coronavirus in the U.S.

DAY TWO HUNDRED AND ELEVEN

Smith sat in the living room of his damaged home, water dripping from the hole in his roof. He heard a knock on the door. A group of neighbors had come to check on him. Frank invited them in, and they toured the destruction. Ms. Mulvaney gasped when she saw his bed.

"It's a miracle you weren't killed."

"I guess it wasn't my time," Frank smiled.

Smith's neighbor Fred offered to call his tree guy who cut down ten trees on his land, obviously at the command of his wife. Ms. Mulvaney brought over some sandwiches later. Frank asked her how her hibiscus was.

"Oh, fine dear," she cooed. "In fact, the only damage in the whole neighborhood was the tree on your house." Her tone appropriately changed to show sympathy for her neighbor.

Frank thanked her for the pimento cheese sandwich even as he thought to himself, *who the hell eats pimento cheese sandwiches anymore?*

Surveying his yard later that day, he did not see one damn hibiscus flower.

1 roll of toilet paper in 01 days.

140 days of social unrest in the U.S.

4,064,019 acres burned in wildfires in the western U.S.

222,277 people have died of the coronavirus in the U.S.

DAY TWO HUNDRED THIRTEEN

The tree men finally came by, removing the trunk from Frank's house. They covered the gaping wound in Frank's roof with plastic because another hurricane was approaching. Three hurricanes in ten days. Lucky for Smith, he did not believe in climate change, otherwise he would have been really upset at the government.

The electricity would not be restored for another day. The food in his refrigerator had spoiled after three days. *What use was electricity anyway?* "Didn't do William Kemmler any good," he mumbled.

Mrs. Mulvaney stopped by each day with more pimento cheese sandwiches. He had grown to like them and told her he would buy some pimentos in the future, whatever they were.

People would walk by and stare at Frank's house. But Frank had ceased caring about any of it. Not hurricanes or wildfires, or pandemics, or social unrest. Frank did not care.

His feet started moving and as he began his pointless circle walk, he thought of punchlines to jokes long-forgotten, or at least long-forgotten by him.

No soap, radio!
I say, could you wobble it a bit? I'm getting it all!
And one of them was a-salted!
It's natural.
Survivors aren't buried!
I'm thinking!
Boo hoo, don't cry!
You really haven't come for the hunting, have you?
Then he lost interest.

1 roll of toilet paper in 25 days.

142 days of social unrest in the U.S.

4,066,019 acres burned in wildfires in the western U.S.

224,082 people have died of the coronavirus in the U.S.

DAY TWO HUNDRED AND SIXTEEN

Hurricane Rufus arrived as projected, in the dark of night. He sat leaning against the hallway wall, drinking Firefly Sweet Tea Vodka straight out of the bottle, and looking into his destroyed bedroom until he could bear it no longer. He shut the door and tried to sleep on the couch. That lasted fifteen minutes before he started pacing. The wind was howling, and he decided to howl with it.

He noticed that he could howl louder than the wind inside his house. He was in a competitive mood, so he went out into the storm to howl in the hurricane's home court. The wind ripped off the screen door as he opened it. It abruptly stopped when it hit the neighbor's fence. *That's a good sign*, he thought.

"Howl," he yelled at the wind and the wind howled back.

"I swear, by thee, I foreswear." The joke was lost on the wind, which had never seen any Bill Murray movies.

He continued in a more desperate manner, bordering on honesty. "Why? Why is all this happening? Is there some purpose? Some grand plan? Will we all, one day, get it? My God! You have done it right! What a stroke of genius! Or will we end our lives in confusion and darkness, dying in ignorance as we lived our lives?"

Smith was enjoying himself. Screaming questions that only the Great God Almighty could hear and understand. God's answer was silence, or was his answer the treacherous swirling wind that took peaceful, well-organized lives and ripped them apart?

And God appeared to Smith in the shape of a pimento cheese sandwich and answered:

"Yell all you want, little man. See what good it does you! You disgust me with all your whimpering! Accept your suffering, like the rest of them. What if you were born blind? Or without a foot? Or a head? Lots of people are born without heads and they get along happily by most reports."

Smith wondered if he had ever seen a headless man at the office, getting along fine or otherwise. He did not want to challenge the all-powerful pimento cheese sandwich on the point. The heavenly father seemed a little annoyed. No need to bother him any further. Besides, Frank was soaked and finding it hard to breathe with the eighty mile-per-hour winds battering him.

He made his way slowly up the steps, holding tightly onto the handrail. At the top stair, the rail broke. Repairing the banister was high on Smith's to-do list, number thirteen in fact. He had not taken care

of the twelve in front of the handrail either, too busy
pacing and making lists. Smith fell with the rail, hitting his head on the unfinished stone path, (which was
number sixty-two on his to-do list) knocking himself
unconscious.

1 roll of toilet paper in 20 days.

145 days of social unrest in the U.S.

**4,069,019 acres burned in wildfires in the western
U.S.**

**225,675 people have died of the coronavirus in the
U.S.**

DAY TWO HUNDRED TWENTY-THREE

It was a week since Smith smacked his head during the third hurricane. Were there three or four? He still felt foggy. He wandered aimlessly, lost in his own home. Smith did not have breakfast. He did not check his email over a morning cup of coffee. He did not set the microwave timer at 22:22. He just paced in his walk circle, shouting at the walls.

Going to see my little baby there. She's stretched out on a long, white table. Well, she looks so good, so cold, so fair.

Lizard crawling on her icy corpse. You want the heat. Hide in the oven. Bastard, shit, bitch, bastard. Lilly, Lilly, where is that dog? The answer is in the toilet paper. That is where you find all the answers!

Frozen peas and frozen sprouts, tips me over and spills me out. Bastard.

Strange fruit hanging from the poplar trees. Dragonfly, dragonfly get out of my house! Here's a shortcut. No need to worry, the deal is done. Direct from China! Don't need your buzzing. Your thousand, thousand eyes. Stop looking at me.

Lilly, where are you girl? Why did you leave me? Why did you go?

1 roll of toilet paper 15 days.

150 days of social unrest in the U.S.

4,081,019 acres burned in wildfires in the western U.S.

230,478 people have died of the coronavirus in the U.S.

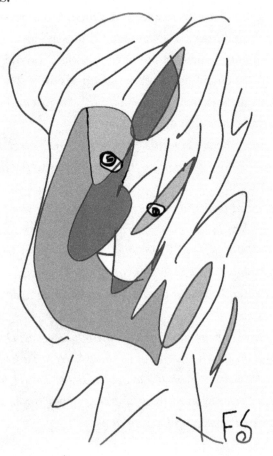

DAY TWO HUNDRED THIRTY-TWO

Election day. Frank Smith did not vote. He walked around his broken home and discussed important subjects with himself.

Probably better not to vote under these circum-stances. Mobs do not understand the ways of our leaders. Hooligans fill the streets causing trouble. Terrorists to the right and left, but they are all good people.

Frank thought they lived in a society that elevated psychopaths to heroes and then wondered why the world was falling apart. *Lucky thing the boards are still up. People think the place is deserted. Probably best that way.*

Children of nobility. First son inherits title and most possessions, and the second son joins the mili-tary. Huh, me in the military! Third son joins the priesthood. Keep those peasants in line.

Frank read a study once that suggested that rich people were less empathetic than the poor because poor people needed each other to survive, whereas rich people could just pay for their survival.

Frank wished everyone would leave him alone.

1 roll of toilet paper in 04 days.

161 days of social unrest in the U.S.*

4,089,019 acres burned in wildfires in the western U.S.

238,577 people have died of the coronavirus in the U.S.

 * After Election Day, the protests against police brutality were overshadowed by protests about the stolen election. But protests were protests and the unrest continued.

DAY TWO HUNDRE FIFTY-THREE

Frank noticed something strange today. His phone clock and his atomic wall clock had different times. Not by hours or minutes, but by seconds. He shut off his phone and restarted it. The wall clock was still eighteen seconds ahead. He changed the batteries in the clock. The clock was still eighteen seconds ahead. *Weren't they getting the same signal from some top-secret government organization somewhere? Shouldn't all clocks be getting the same signal?*

Frank stopped walking his circle walk. He stared at the wall clock. *How could this be?*

He read an article once about a financial company that was doing something to something which gave them a half second head start on the trading floor. They made billions of dollars with that little advantage. What advantage would eighteen seconds give a company? People who could manipulate time by even a second or two could control the world.

Maybe it was a movie he saw. Somebody could see a few seconds into the future. No, that wasn't it, it was a bank robbery, a corporate safe, or the stock exchange. But it wasn't a movie. It was definitely real life. And someone was definitely trying to take over the world. Smith did not remember if there were ever any consequences. *The rich never pay the piper.*

But this was not a millisecond. This was eighteen seconds! Frank walked to his front door and parted the curtain slightly. He peered into the street. Fred was mowing his lawn, not realizing that the world was about to be taken over by some nefarious group of financial-computer-nerd-hackers who had manipulated the top-secret-government-time-controlling-organization into sending out erroneous time signals. *Fred is mowing the grass while the world is ending! Schmuck.*

Frank let the curtain fall. He smiled as he turned into his hallway to continue his walk. He knew he had lost some time as he uncovered the plot, but he could always make it up later.

He hadn't made it around once before he felt his heart pounding. He held up his left hand, which shook violently. It always started with his left hand. His right hand began its convulsions soon after. He was relieved when he made it into the living room and could lay down on the rug until the shaking passed.

He faced upwards and watched the fan slowly turn clockwise. It needed to be dusted and Frank was directly beneath it. At any moment, a chunk of dust would break off and slowly float downward, hitting his face.

He closed his eyes, waiting for the end to come. But it did not come. God was not that merciful.

After ten minutes, Frank's pulse had returned to normal. After an hour, he was brave enough to open his eyes. The clump of dust still hung precariously from the fan. He should put cleaning fans on his list. *That would show them. Stick it to the fan!*

Frank rolled onto his hands and knees and crept to the couch. He picked up his A. Summer collection of poems.

"I once" by A. Summer

I once loved a girl
but she loved a pharmacist
there was no reason
love finds a way
he hurt her
but she loved him just the same
she stayed with me
until her heart mended
and when she was strong enough
she left me
for him
to be hurt again
and when she was strong enough
she broke my heart
not because she wanted to
but because she did not care
we only care for those we love

for those we don't, we don't.
it's easy to be cruel
to those we don't,
when yesterday we did.

1 roll of toilet paper in 21 days.

182 days of social unrest in the U.S.

4,104,019 acres burned in wildfires in the western U.S.

265,917 people have died of the coronavirus in the U.S.

DAY TWO HUNDRED SIXTY-ONE

S mith could not remember what day it was. He looked at his phone. The calendar displayed symbols he no longer understood, so he sang a song.

> Three little birds can rhyme a lot
> cooking in the iron pot
> tweet, tweet, tweet, tweet, tweet, too, too
> nothing else to say or do!
>
> tweet tweet twiddle de tweet bum bum
> drink more vodka, drink more rum
> do not fret and do not frown
> as your demons pull you down
>
> life is joyful, life is free
> when it gets the best of me
> pain is over, pain is done
> close your eyes here comes the sun
>
> tweet tweet tweedle dum tweet TomTom
> tweet tweet twiddle cause you da bomb
> tweedle, tweedle, tweedle dee
> this will be the death of me

Trumpdy Dumpty wanted a wall
Trumpdy Dumpty had a great fall
Marbleless Rudy and the rest of his men
couldn't make Trumpdy the president again

1 roll of toilet paper in 19 days.
190 days of social unrest in the U.S.
4,114,019 acres burned in wildfires in the western
U.S. The wildfire season ended in the U.S. around
this time.
279,911 people have died of the coronavirus in the
U.S.

DAY TWO HUNDRED SIXTY-SEVEN

Smith walked around his house aimlessly. He felt the need to clean something but only managed to move piles of things from one place to another, never putting anything away. *Why should I?* he eventually thought. *This is all my stuff. I need my stuff right where it is. If I move my stuff, I won't be able to find it. What if I needed this stapler? But I moved it, you see. I wouldn't know where it was and that would be bad. That would be horrific! With all the terrible things happening in the world, can't I have my stapler where I want it? Can't I have anything the way I want it?*

This last question stopped him. Nothing moved him for an hour. He heard a distant sound in his brain. It was like a voice too far away to be heard with clarity. But soon he found himself humming. When the music was clearer, he began to sing.

I've got a lovely bunch of coconuts.

Here they are standing in a row!

Big ones, fat ones, kids who play on tops,

Small ones, thin ones,

Even kids with chickenpox,

Love hot dogs, Armor hot dogs,

The dogs kids love to bite!

Very nice! A pretty ditty! One must always sepa-rate the pain from the pills. He sang again:

As I walked out on the streets of Laredo.

As I walked out in Laredo one day

I saw a young cowboy, wrapped all in white linen.

Shot in a gunfight for the love of Sally Day!

Poor dumb bastard...I've never known a man who believed in love that couldn't be deceived by a woman who believed in nothing.

Which inspired him to sing again:

My girl's a corker

She's a New Yorker

I buy her everything to keep her in style

She's got a pair of hips

Just like two battleships

Hey boys, that's where my money goes.

1 roll of toilet paper in 20 days.

196 days of social unrest in the U.S.

293,378 people have died of the coronavirus in the U.S.

DAY TWO HUNDRED EIGHTY-ONE

Smith found himself in the town square, staring at the American flag at 2:30 in the morning in his pajamas. He had no idea how he got to the town square to look at the flag at 2:30 in the morning in his pajamas. If truth be told, he did not even know he was there until a police officer came up to him and asked him if he was all right.

Smith didn't reply. He did not look at the officer, just kept staring at the flag.

A few people who stumbled out of the local bars stopped to see what had happened. Several pulled out their cellphones and began to live stream the event, as had become the custom. They hoped for bloodshed. *They always secretly hope for bloodshed.* After repeated attempts to get Frank Smith to focus, the officer called for backup and Smith was arrested. He put up no resistance, just kept looking at the flag.

Frank shared his cell with an African American. The man was in his thirties and seemed intimidating at first glance. Both men were silent for a while. His cellmate sat studying his hands as if they were the cause of his imprisonment. Frank stood, continuing to stare at the flag that was no longer in front of him.

"You go to any of the protests?" asked the man, looking at Frank's wrist.

Frank was confused until he realized he was wearing the Black Lives Matter wristband.

"No," Frank said nervously. "I just bought a wristband."

"You think that's going to help?"

"Probably not. Should I take it off?"

"No, man, leave it on. Can't hurt."

Frank felt relieved. "What are you in here for?" He hoped it was not for some violent crime.

"Cop said my tail light was out. I told him I was going to get a tail light. He didn't believe me. I was in the goddamn auto store parking lot! Said I was getting aggressive and called for backup. Lucky I'm not dead. What did you do?"

"I looked at the flag in the town square."

"When did you do that?"

"An hour ago."

"In your pajamas?"

"Yes."

"In the middle of the night?"

"Yes."

"With Crocs?"

"Yes."

"If you were black, you'd be dead."

"I'm glad I'm not black then."

Frank immediately ealized how bad that sounded.

The man looked at him and smiled. "That's all right, man. I understand. It's tough to be a black man in America."

"How do you deal with the hate every day?"

"A minute at a time. Were you afraid when you saw me?"

"I was." Frank felt ashamed and took off his wristband. "I don't deserve to wear this. Do you want it?"

"No, I don't need to be reminded that black lives matter. You keep it, 'cause from the looks of it, you got a lot of shit to work through. But do me a favor."

"What is it?"

"Don't take it off until there's justice for everyone."

"That might be a long time."

"Probably, but maybe if you did something besides wearing that wristband it wouldn't be that long."

His cellmate rose and walked to the other side of the cell.

In the morning, Frank was brought before the judge, who asked him why he was staring at the flag.

Smith looked down at his feet and replied in a soft voice, "I don't know how we got here."

The judge asked if he had someone at home who could pick him up. Smith said no. The judge asked if he could get home all right. Smith said, "I believe so."

After looking at him for a while, the judge said, "I don't know how it came about in this country, that a man could be arrested for looking at our flag, but you did create a public nuisance and therefore I will fine you $500 and let you go on your own recognizance."

"Thank you, your honor. I have been turned down for unemployment and I am in the process of appealing, could I pay the fine then?"

The judge looked at Smith and dismissed the case.

1 roll of toilet paper in 25 days.

210 days of social unrest in the U.S.

322,585 people have died of the coronavirus in the U.S.

DAY TWO HUNDRED EIGHTY-TWO

From the video posted online, the press got wind of Smith's arrest and reported on the incident with great relish. The right called him a socialist threat to the country. The left thought he was an alt-right racist. Everyone hated Smith.

They camped out in front of his house. Ms. Mulvaney brought sandwiches to the crowd. Frank noticed that he was down to twelve rolls of toilet paper and started to get anxious about it. He would have liked to have gone to the store and get some more but he did not want to walk through the crowd. This was his fifteen minutes of fame.

He threw a roll of toilet paper at the protestors.

1 roll of toilet paper in 04 days.
211 days of social unrest in the U.S.
325,097 people have died of the coronavirus in the U.S.

DAY TWO HUNDRED NINETY-ONE

....

The crowd outside his home left. First the right left. And then the left left; no one to annoy with their signs printed on recycled paper. Frank kept going back to his front door to peek out the window until he realized that he missed them. There was something comforting about the anger and death threats.

Mr. K. ended badly.

1 roll of toilet paper in 05 days.
220 days of social unrest in the U.S.
383,779 people have died of the coronavirus in the U.S.

DAY TWO HUNDRED NINETY-SIX

Frank thought that believing the election was sto-len from Trump was like believing in God. Even though there was no earthly proof that God existed they still had to believe in him. All those people must be very holy, although Frank couldn't understand why someone who loved God so much would break into the capital wearing a camp Auschwitz shirt or with weapons. *Weren't they all supposed to beat their weapons into plowshares?* It was all too confusing; that's why Frank didn't believe in anything.

Frank had a sad thought: *We are in a prison of our own making, without knowledge of the crime but believing we should be punished.* And then he wrote a poem to commemorate the day's events.

> The long forgotten Mr. A.
> Was taken off on Wed-nes-day,
> Without a fuss.
> The people all will dance and sing
> As Mr. A. dies in the ring,
> Stabbed gladly thus
> He must have erred against the state

There's always room for more debate
As Mr. Boss is fanning the flame!
As Mr. Boss is playing his game!

Both good and bad are swept away
And ignorance is free to play,
Makes quite a scene
The people all will shout and swear
A legislator's over there,
Let's all be mean!

Their call for vengeance is quite loud
And many lies whip up the crowd
As Mr. Boss is fanning the flame!
As Mr. Boss is playing his game!

1 roll of toilet paper in 01 days.
225 days of social unrest in the U.S
362,144 people have died of the coronavirus in the U.S.

DAY THREE HUNDRED AND TWO

He had thrown the picture against the wall years ago, the final punctuation for the ended relationship. It had fallen behind the couch in the guest room and lived there, for years, along with the broken glass.

He had not cleaned the room since that day. But he could not go outside because the protestors were back and the roofers were walking around his house as they did their repairs, so he locked himself in the guest room and cleaned.

After spending two hours cleaning the surfaces, shredding paper and vacuuming, Frank decided to clean under the couch. He saw the shards of glass on the floor and the photograph facing up. Frank picked it up and looked at her. She was beautiful. He loved her once. He was not sure if his feelings were gone, but they were different.

He had stopped taking photos after she left, tired of lonely landscapes, dying flowers, and selfies taken from strange angles. As he picked up the glass, he cut his index finger. This would be another scar from the relationship. He found a used frame. He put the old picture in the new frame and placed it gently on the table. He didn't know whether it would last there, his feelings ambiguous, his thoughts confused.

Throwing a fragile object is a grand gesture, but we eventually must clean up our messes.

1 roll of toilet paper in 20 days.
231 days of social unrest in the U.S.
389,839 people have died of the coronavirus in the U.S.

DAY THREE HUNDRED AND THREE

The President gave a speech. He seemed like a robot, like someone was controlling him, like that episode of Star Trek, the original series, where some guy went to some planet and modeled their society after the Nazis. Then he'd been drugged when some evil guy wanted the planet for his own. Anyway, Trump seemed like he was drugged...or speaking in code.

Frank downloaded his speech and a transcript and made a mark whenever Trump paused. *By using the Von Hammerschnitzel method of decipherication that I learned in college, I can figure this out.* Frank came up with the following message:

"THE SOCIALISTS HAVE TAKEN CONTROL OF THE GOVERNMENT. THE ELECTION WAS A FRAUD. RISE UP, MY MINIONS. I LIKE CHEESE."

Frank agreed with Trump, but who didn't like cheese?

1 roll of toilet paper in 08 days.

242 days of social unrest in the U.S.

393,913 people have died of the coronavirus in the U.S.

DAY THREE HUNDRED ELEVEN

....

F rank read the last poem in A. Summer's book.

"afraid"

i'm not afraid of dying
because there's no one in my life
i'm afraid of losing.

Frank wondered if there was anyone in A. Summer's life that he was afraid of losing.

Was that the criteria for not caring? Just being alone? Do we need people to hold onto, to laugh with, to cry with? Isn't life better without these emotional ties? Why cling in quiet desperation to people who will leave us?

Frank looked at the photographs in his house. His three girls, Sally with chocolate sauce, Sarah in her tutu, the four of them in New York, Sandra and Sally, Lilly, Smith in a college theatrical, parents in an art gallery, his father's parents, his mother's parents, his parents, Sarah at the big game, parents.

Photographs were a way of telling others, *I once had something special. I've had my time. I've had enough.*

He looked at his bookcases. Bookcase one, bookcase two, bookcase three, bookcase four. *Is this the sum total of my life, fifty pictures and a couple hundred old books? A week after my death, a dumpster will be dropped off and all this stuff carted away. Why have I collected so much meaningless crap?*

He thought of the hidden boxes in his attic. Were these objects meant to prove that Smith's life had value? The poet held onto people until there were no people left to hold. Smith held onto objects because objects could never hurt him.

He thought about that red ball on top of that high rope in his gym class. If he'd only touched the ball, then maybe he would have tried harder in love. No matter how many times his heart was broken maybe he would have tried one more time and succeeded.

Because that was what those people did, those ball touchers. They never stopped trying.

1 roll of toilet paper in 13 days.
241 days of social unrest in the U.S.
420,298 people have died of the coronavirus in the U.S.

DAY THREE HUNDRED TWENTY-EIGHT

Frank Smith laid down on his bed. He was having difficulty breathing. Maybe the virus had finally got him. He left a text for his eldest daughter to visit him tomorrow, explaining that he had something to share with her. Smith had not spoken to any of his children in more than two months. He had nothing to share. There was nothing left...to...share.

He rubbed his left arm. Must be his frozen shoulder again. He closed his eyes. They were hard to keep open anymore. And just for a moment, he remembered a woman.

Later that day, Frank's first unemployment check arrived.

The phone rang, but Frank Smith did not answer.

257 days of social unrest in the U.S.
474,933 people have died of the coronavirus in the U.S.

O *ver half a million people have died of the corona-*
virus in the United States in a little over one year...

AUTHOR NOTES AND GRATITUDE

Some things should be clarified; some people must be thanked. Let me begin with the gratitude:

I would like to thank the members of the Main Street Reads writer's group; Carol Webster, Christina Sinisi, Drew Bogert, Karin Kaltofen, Patricia Frisch, Regina Williams, Doug Hankel, Sandra Brundage, Syril Levin Kline, and Kathleen Varn. Their insight and encouragement on a weekly basis made sharing not only helpful but fun.

I would also like to thank my friends and family members who read and gave me feedback on the various drafts of this work or gave me encouragement on my journey. They let me know that even though I was alone in my isolation during the pandemic, I was always loved. So, thank you Dave, Jill, Eliza, Juliet, and Helena. Thank you Darlene Waring, Gina Causey, Megan Stauch and Wendy Gregg.

Finally, I would like to thank Shari Stauch, owner of Main Street Reads, creator of the Main Street Reads writer's group, driving force behind Writers Win, my mentor and friend. Her tireless efforts in turning this interesting idea into the novel before you were awe-inspiring. The lessons she taught me about the art and the business of writing will never be forgotten. And the joy and laughter we shared through the process made times when tough decisions had to be made more palatable.

And here are some notes regarding items mentioned within the text, beginning with the art:

- Smith in a college theatrical (production photo from "The Mad Woman of Chaillot")
- Van Gogh (Starry Night)
- (Jennifer) Harkleroad a talented painter in the South Carolina low country
- Birdlady (artist unknown, initials BG),
- Vincent (Self-portrait of Vincent Van Gogh)
- MacHeath (Poster from Three Penny Opera)
- Life is Beautiful (poster with pastel chrysanthemums)
- Van Gogh (Café Terrace at Night),
- Of Mice and Men (College theatrical)
- Whirling stairs (In courtyard of the James Joyce home, Dublin, Ireland)
- Trinity Library (Trinity College, Dublin, Ireland)
- Homeless Jesus (at Christ Church Cathedral, Dublin, Ireland)

Books noted in the story in order of appearance:
- *Man in the Holocene* by Max Frisch
- *Krapp's Last Tape* by Samuel Beckett
- *Island of Statues* by W.B. Yeats

- ***Stephen King On Writing*** by Stephen King
- ***No Exit*** by Sartre
- ***Hemingway On Writing*** by Hemingway
- ***A Walk in the Valley*** by A.F. Winter
- ***Howl*** by Allen Ginsberg
- ***Cinderella's End*** by A.F. Winter
- ***The Trial*** by Franz Kafka
- ***The Good Soldier Sjeck*** by Jaroslav Hašek
- ***The Stranger*** by Albert Camus
- ***Through the Looking Glass*** by Lewis Carrol
- ***Fantasius Mallare*** by Ben Hecht
- ***Siddhartha*** by Hermann Hesse
- ***The Tibetan Book of the Dead*** Various

Credit also to:

- *"I met a girl who sang the blues and asked her for some happy news."* From the hit single, "American Pie" by Don McLean.
- William Kemmler was the first person to be electrocuted after receiving the death penalty.
- Information about nuclear destruction from Nuke Map by Alex Wellerstein: https://nuclear-secrecy.com/nukemap/
- Coronavirus death toll, numbers from https://www.worldometers.info/coronavirus/country/us/
- Wildfire acres destroyed statistics taken from https://en.wikipedia.org/wiki/2020_Western_United_States_wildfire_season.

ABOUT THE AUTHOR

A.F. Winter has written books on the theatre and several plays, winning the South Carolina Playwright's Festival. This is his fifth novel. He has also written several books of poetry. He lives near Charleston, SC with his dog, Millie and is overjoyed when one of his three exceptional daughters comes to visit. Learn more at www.afwinter.com.

Other Books by A.F. Winter

Theatre Builds Character

The Actor, the Script, and the Ox

A Walk in the Valley

I Am Vincent

Happy

Cinderella's End

Ireland in Black and White (with Sam Beckett)

Sleeping With Macbeth

In Love's Twilight

She Does It All